RESCUE
HEART

A LOVE STORY

TANE McCLURE

Quantity sales special discounts are available on quantity purchases by corporations, associations, and others. For details, contact the publisher at the address above.

Orders by U.S. trade bookstores and wholesalers. Email info@ BeyondPublishing.net

The Beyond Publishing Speakers Bureau can bring authors to your live event. For more information or to book an event contact the Beyond Publishing Speakers Bureau speak@BeyondPublishing.net

The Author can be reached directly at BeyondPublishing.net

Manufactured and printed in the United States of America distributed globally by BeyondPublishing.net

BEYOND
PUBLISHING

New York | Los Angeles | London | Sydney

ISBN Hardcover: 978-1-637922-28-6

DEDICATION

To Kai.

My "Rescue Heart."

ACKNOWLEDGEMENTS

Thank you to my family for your love and support. Special thanks to Tyke Caravelli for helping me build the story of Rescue Heart as a screenplay; De De Cox for inspiring me to turn that screenplay into a book; my publisher Michael Butler for believing in me. And with deep gratitude I would like to thank L.I.F.E. Animal Rescue for saving my dog Kai from the Dog Meat market in Thailand, and bringing her to the United States along with hundreds of other dogs in need, that deserve kindness, love and a happy home.

CONTENTS

PROLOGUE

Nina choked down another shot of tequila to numb the world around her. The fights had always disgusted her. The barking, the snarling, the jeering of the crowd, Savin's voice crowing across the room whenever his pick got a bite in, the shrill cries of the losing dog resisting his inevitable defeat. The sounds alone were enough to drive her away from the ring and up to the bar. Never mind the sight of the carnage which drew the eager crowd of drunken gamblers and spectators.

That night she had made the grievous mistake of looking into one of the dog carriers as it was brought to the floor of the ring. A beautiful, slender Shepherd mix had peered back at her with an intelligence that made her gasp. He had a golden-brown coat with a dusting of golden freckles around his forehead and muzzle, giving him the face of youth and innocence.

There was a wolfishness to him that reminded her of a wolfdog her mother had owned back at the reservation when she was very little. This flash of nostalgia combined with the almost-humanlike look he had given her on the way to the ring made her feel an immediate sense of connection to the poor creature. Her stomach twisted as another desperate cry, accompanied by equal cheers and defeated groans, echoed from the arena. She was sure the yelp had come from the golden dog from the carrier.

Another shot of tequila raced down her throat, the burning barely noticeable, and she realized she had risen from the bar and turned to face the ring, her hands balled into fists. The dog released another cry, even more pitiful than the last. He was giving up, she could feel it. From across the room, she saw Savin standing on a short, metal podium raised slightly above the ring. One hand clenched a fistful of hundreds while the other waved a retractable cattle prod. Savin swung the cattle prod down into the ring at the beautiful, golden dog. He hated to lose and the dog was going to get the brunt of his rage.

"Get up you lazy sack of shit! I said *fight, damn it!*" Savin roared. His eyes were wild and his speech heavy, the mark of too many toxins already coursing through his system.

The dog was barely recognizable. His gorgeous coat was completely matted with blood and dirt, tongue lolling out the side of his mouth, deep gashes apparent across his face. His freckles that Nina had admired earlier were now mixed with flecks of blood, hardly even distinguishable. He had collapsed in the corner, shaking with fear, his tail curled up between his back legs. His opponent, a grey-blue muscular Pitbull nearly twice his size, seemed to be taking his time finishing him off. He paced the other side of the ring slowly, methodically. Savin's cattle prod made contact and the dog yelped, his tail driving farther between his legs, his shaking becoming more intense. Savin repeated his assault twice more. By the third strike, the poor dog no longer had the energy to cry out.

"Stop it! Please just stop! Why do you have to fight them? *Stop it!*"

Nina took a step back, surprised by the force of her own voice. The crowd quieted down, confused, and turned to face Nina. In seconds, Savin had shoved the money in his pocket, leapt down from his podium, and crossed the room to the bar. His face was twisted and red with rage. Before Nina could make a move to escape, he was on top of her. The scent of his stale tobacco and harsh cologne was overwhelming as he bared down on her. With one hand, he grabbed her by the neck and pushed her back against the bar. Nina felt something scrape her cheek and realized Savin was holding the tip of the cattle prod against her jaw.

"Who the *hell* do you think you're talking to?" Savin hissed. "These are *my* dogs. Mine!"

Savin bellowed into Nina's face, spraying her with the remnants of his chew. "You are mine, so you should know, I do what I want with what is *mine!*"

Heart beating in her throat, Nina stared back into the vicious face of the man who once claimed to love her. It was hard to believe now. Impossible. Maybe Savin was thinking the same thing, as he tightened his fist, threatening to squeeze the life out of her. He looked into her pained yet beautiful deep brown eyes. His knuckles twisted and tangled in her sleek long black hair rubbing against her soft amber-brown skin.

Nina was undeniably a stunning young woman. To keep her in line, Savin liked to remind her that she was just a *nothing*, Native American girl. No one cared if she disappeared, beauty or not. But tonight, for whatever the reason, Savin decided to loosen his death grip on her neck. Perhaps, he noticed how difficult it was for Nina to breathe, and he had decided he wasn't ready to throw her away. Not yet. His eyes softened just a bit as he released her.

Without turning back to the crowd, Savin announced, "I concede. Separate the dogs."

He shot a death glare at Nina before turning slowly to address the crowd and throw his money towards the general direction of his opponent. "And just so you all know...it has *nothing* to do with her."

Nina sucked in a deep breath, relief flooding through her, both for herself and the shepherd. She knew Savin was trying to save face, but she didn't care. She struggled to her feet, pushing the tears of fear and relief back.

Savin took two large steps toward her and pulled Nina forward by the collar of her shirt, their noses almost touching.

"If you ever embarrass me like that again..." Savin clicked the cattle prod just inches from Nina's cheek. "As for your friend in the ring: since he can't fight now, he's only of worth to me as a bait dog. And to think his suffering could have ended tonight if you had just kept your mouth shut. Tsk, tsk..."

A malicious grin spread across Savin's face as he watched Nina realize that in attempting to save him, she had just sentenced the dog to a horrific death. Nina closed her eyes in agony as the reality of her entrapment became brutally clear. She was trapped, just like the beautiful dog she tried to rescue.

CHAPTER 1

—— RUN ——

The drone was silent except for a low hum. With only a glint of the light of dawn etching the New Mexico desert skyline, the drone flew stealth-fully over a Navajo Reservation with tattered homes and broken down old cars, and then up and over a mountain ridge.

Finally, it found its mark as it hovered over the sandy drive leading up to James Savin's mansion, a camera attached to its base swiveled slowly from side to side. Detecting no one in the immediate vicinity, the drone proceeded up the drive. It slowly cruised past several low-lying buildings, an assortment of trucks and cars parked across the property, and the mansion itself. It was a stylish, well maintained building with a sandy exterior and a dark red-shingled roof. The stillness in the air created a serene sort of environment, although the inside of the mansion was anything but.

The morning sun cresting the horizon sparkled against the mansion's windows. The drone took a moment to scan the front of the mansion before moving past it, toward a dreary, slate-gray warehouse in the back.

A large sliding door at the end of the warehouse stood ajar, leaving plenty of space for the drone to slip inside. Once inside, the drone stopped dead, almost as if it were stunned by what it saw. Rows of cages lined the walls, each containing a different wild animal. Bobcats, deer, coyotes, a lone buffalo, and more stood, cramped in rusting cages. The drone took its time gliding down the aisle, making sure to capture each animal on camera. Most were listless and made no move to acknowledge the drone. One bobcat gave a feeble growl but made no effort to back up the weak threat. Interspersed amongst the wild animals were a wide variety of dogs ranging from Pitbulls to German Shepherds to Dobermans to Rhodesian Ridgebacks. Some bore old, deep scars and others nursed fresh wounds. While grisly, none of the injuries were too severe. These dogs were the victors, after all.

At the very end of the warehouse stood a large cage with a group of smaller dogs smeared with colorful paint. The drone slowed to a halt before the pitiful group. Terriers, Chihuahuas, Beagles, Australian shepherds, and all kinds of mutts were huddled in the cage. The lens on the drone's camera tipped to the side, taking notice of a dog outside of the cage that looked just as pitiful as those were, but was not covered in paint. Tied to a post by the backdoor, the golden dog licked at his many wounds.

The drone stopped advancing and hovered in place when the dog cowered and scuttled backwards at its approach. The hum of the drone sounded far too familiar to that of the electric cattle prod.

Swiveling back toward the entrance, the drone made its retreat, flying back up the center aisle at a far more rapid pace. Back out the front door, the drone wound its way between a shiny new Tesla and a rusty pickup truck. The drone turned its camera back toward the truck, but only for a moment. Nearly to the edge of the property, the drone braked hard, skidding through the air. The camera whipped back toward the mansion, lens flexing to zoom in on a downstairs window. The house was still no longer. Nimble fingers shifted the lower half of the window up in one smooth, fluid motion. Nina's petite silhouette appeared in the gap.

Hanging motionless in the air, as if the machine itself were surprised by this turn of events, the drone captured every second of the silent escape. Nina swung her legs out of the window and dropped to the ground, then she turned and reached back in to pull out a duffel bag and backpack. She had started running before she had fully pulled on the straps of her back pack. After a moment, her destination became clear; she was running full tilt toward the rusty pickup truck. Maintaining a safe distance, the drone followed suit.

***

Visions flashed through Nina's mind with every step she took. The sound of her sneakers crunching across the desert sand snapped her from one memory to the next. None of it seemed real. Even now, her escape nearly complete, Nina had a hard time fathoming what she had done.

It had been relatively simple in retrospect. Years of living on Savin's compound as something more like living furniture than a live-in girlfriend had allowed her to develop a detailed knowledge of the place. She knew where all the bodies were buried, both figuratively and literally. While an outsider would have had trouble navigating Savin's maze-like mansion, finding places to hide items necessary for her escape, or locating where Savin kept his cash, Nina was intimately familiar with all of those things.

It helped that Savin's bodyguards had little respect for Nina. They let key details about Savin's operation slip all the time. She knew who brought the drugs across the border, she knew who the middlemen were, she knew where they stopped for gas on the distribution route, and the names of their favorite prostitutes from every state. She also knew how much money was kept on the premises, where it was kept, and how it was protected. She didn't have the whole picture, but she could make use of what she did have. The men never expected that she was paying attention. They sure as hell never thought she could or would use any of that information.

She had slipped out of bed just before dawn. The gin and tonics she had served Savin the night before had contained twice as much gin as she usually used. Even so, she took great care to cross the room quietly and felt pure terror cut through her chest when the bedroom door creaked open.

She had not greased it enough. Savin grumbled something in his sleep but did not wake, to Nina's immense relief.

Wearing nothing but a t-shirt and underwear, Nina had then made her way to Savin's study, only taking hallways she knew the guards would not be patrolling at that hour. From beneath the couch, Nina retrieved her duffel bag and backpack. The backpack contained pants, a shirt, and a pair of sneakers. Once dressed she moved to Savin's desk and felt around the edge of it for the hidden switch one of the guards had told her about. With a satisfying click, Nina's fingers clamped down on the switch, opening a small compartment with a key inside. The key was for the hidden drawer on an inside panel of Savin's desk the guard, Harold, had said. That was where Savin kept his "liquid assets." Nina removed wads of tightly rolled cash from the drawer and realized as she did so that she was holding more money in her hands than anyone in her family had ever possessed.

With the cash stuffed in the backpack, Nina flung open a cabinet to reveal an assortment of car keys hanging from several dozen hooks. She would have liked to have taken the Tesla. It was quiet, fast, and clean. But she knew that Savin would be after her in a heartbeat. He used the car frequently, and he likely placed more value in the car than he did Nina. No, it would have to be the truck. She hadn't seen that beat up pickup truck over by the garage move in a while. It wouldn't be missed. She snatched the keys, collected her bags, and ran to the back window.

She had just laid her hand against the glass when she heard it: the solid clack of heeled boots against the tiled floor headed her way. Fear swept through her once again. This wasn't right! Cooper wasn't scheduled to patrol the study for another twenty minutes! Her mind spun as she attempted to churn out possible alternative escape routes, but none presented themselves. She was done. She'd never get out the window in time. Even if she did, Cooper would see her.

The sound of radio static made her jump. Cooper's footsteps stopped.

"What was that Harold? You're breaking up man." He sounded frustrated as his muffled voice echoed through the hallway. Nina held her breath, as he wasn't talking but she knew he was still there. After a moment, she could hear fractions of the conversation in between the thumping of Cooper's pacing.

"....the front... motion detectors going... backup..."

The silence was agony but Nina stayed completely still, so when Cooper's next statement rang through the halls with vibrating anger, she nearly jumped out of her skin.

"There's a *breach*? Where are you? Who is it?"

He calmed enough to lower his voice and his footsteps started to sound further away.

"...check the... I think... front gate..."

"I'm headed out front, hold on!"

Nina waited until the sound of Cooper's footsteps had disappeared entirely before she allowed herself to move again. She approached the back window and held her breath as she slowly raised it up. She wasn't totally sure if she had successfully turned off the window alarms the night before. Savin never told her the code, but she had watched him many times. She knew the pattern. As the window creaked up, she exhaled. No alarm had sounded. She maneuvered herself through the open window with ease. It was a straight shot from here. She could taste freedom on the morning breeze.

The back-passenger window of the truck had been left open and she threw the duffel and backpack into the truck without stopping. Adrenaline rocketed through her veins, leaving her hands shaky and clumsy. It took her three tries to fit the key into the car door and two to get it into the ignition. She let out a sigh of relief that sounded more like a whimper when the engine started. The noise triggered another memory. The face of the dog she had angered Savin into sentencing as a bait dog a week prior leapt into her mind with startling clarity. The wolfish demeanor... those human eyes...

Her eyes drifted to the warehouse.

"No. No time. No." She dug her fingers into the steering wheel. The echoes of the dog's cries replayed in her head. The memory of his defeated form, slumped against the side of the ring, unable to move away from the crackling electricity being wielded against him... And his fate would be worse now. No bait dog ever left the ring in one piece. Not with Savin.

Nina beat her fist against the steering wheel then flung the door back open, feet flying across the desert sand.

CHAPTER 2

—— THE DISCOVERY ——

Agent Lianna Cortez, threw her cellphone down on the desk of the surveillance van, unable to hide her anger and disappointment. It landed on a crumpled burger wrapper, a remnant of just one of many meals she'd had to eat in the cramped space. Her partner, Agent Andrew Davis, tore his eyes away from his computer screen for just long enough to catch a glimpse of the scowl on Cortez's face. He shook his head.

"Come on, you knew he would tell us to stand down. This is a surveillance mission. Not a run-in-guns-a-blazin' mission."

Davis' attempt at levity made Cortez roll her eyes. She was fond of the younger agent, even if he made rather corny jokes. "I know we need evidence of the drug ring, but damn..." She tapped on one of the screenshots of the paint covered bait dogs in the warehouse on Davis' second monitor. "It makes me sick to leave them there. I still think we should take him on the animal abuse charges and circle back for the drugs later."

Davis, a bookish looking, smaller framed young man, was packed with brains but little apparent brawn. He nervously pushed his glasses up his nose and shook his head again. "Cortez, you know the second we move on Savin his bosses will make any trace of his involvement disappear. Then we'll have no chance of—"

"Getting Quintero, yes I know. I am painfully well aware," Cortez snapped. Her eyes made their way back over to the live feed from the drone as it flitted across the brightening landscape. She scowled at the mansion's golden façade. Its stillness mocked her, like a silent perp smirking at her from across the interrogation table.

Cortez, at 38 years old, was considered a top notch, hard-hitting FBI agent. She was still single, and quite attractive. She should probably have more suitors, except for the fact that she could outrun and outgun many of her male counterparts at the agency to their weaker ego's absolute annoyance. During her career, she had her fair share of hits as well as some big misses, but she wasn't planning on missing a single thing on this case. This could potentially be her biggest case ever.

She watched the drone monitor like a hawk. For a moment, the flurry of movement by a first-floor window registered as nothing more than a trick of the light.

"Stop the drone!" she cried, realizing this was no illusion.

Davis braked hard. Cortez could hear the powerful little engine whine with the effort of halting in midair.

"There," Cortez breathed, finger hovering over the image of Nina clambering out the mansion window. The pair watched in awed silence as Nina gathered her bags and took off running.

"Who is that? Tell me we know who that is," Cortez whispered, eyes never leaving the drone footage.

Davis clicked open a series of files. A myriad of faces flashed across his computer screen. "No... I have no idea who she is."

"Then I guess we'd better find out. Follow her."

"But Supervisor Stone told us to return to the office—"

A sharp look from Cortez put a stop to any further objection from Davis. The drone performed a 180 and flew after Nina.

The agents watched as Nina's shadowy figure cut straight across the compound, directly for a beat-up pickup truck near the property line.

"Interesting choice," Davis remarked. "I have to say, if I were fleeing a vicious drug lord in the early morning, I would have opted for taking his Tesla."

"It's a smart choice," Cortez replied. "Assuming she is running, she picked the car he's least likely to notice is missing. Clever girl."

Davis furrowed his brow. "She's not leaving. Why isn't she leaving?"

Both agents leaned in closer to the monitor. Nina's shadow was visible behind the wheel. The rumble of the truck's engine was audible on the drone's feed, yet Nina did not put the car in drive. After a long moment, Nina punched the steering wheel and leapt from the car.

"What on Earth! Follow her!" Cortez gave Davis' shoulder a tight squeeze.

Davis kept the drone at a safe distance and continued after Nina as she raced to the warehouse. Davis halted the drone, uncertain. They couldn't follow her in without being discovered.

"There was a vent in the back. Above the bait dogs."

Davis grinned. Cortez knew next to nothing about technology, but in every other respect she paid attention to detail. Of course she had noticed the vent.

Davis looped the drone down to the back of the warehouse and ventured as close to the vent as he dared, focusing the lens of the craft as he did so. From their perch by the vent, the agents watched through the slots as Nina crept towards the mix that had been tied to a post by the back door.

"Oh, that must be her dog," Cortez sighed. "How awful."

Nina reached to untie the rope from the dog's collar and was immediately forced to retreat as he snapped at her.

"Or maybe *not* her dog," Davis quipped.

The agents watched as Nina approached the dog again, palms raised in a soothing manner. She made her way around the dog, this time going for the end of the rope tied to the post. She gives the rope a tug, but the dog refuses to budge.

"While she's messing around with the dog, circle back to the truck. I want to make sure we get those plates before she takes off."

Davis shot away from the vent and swept across the expanse of desert in front of the mansion, back towards the truck.

Bang!

Both agents jumped at the noise. Davis pivoted the drone's camera to face the front door of the mansion, where two rough looking men dressed in black now stood. The shorter of the two held a rifle with a scope attached. He had lowered the gun to check and see if he had hit his target. Realizing he failed, he raised the rifle once again.

"Get us out of here!" Cortez's voice was razor sharp as she knew if they lost the drone, their already weak evidence would be non-existent.

Davis shot the drone skyward, higher and higher until he knew that the drone was nothing more than a pin prick in the sky to the men below.

"Oh, what the hell man. We gotta get out of here! I know I said I wanted to spend more time away from my desk, but you know what doesn't happen at my desk? Guns. Guns don't happen at my desk," Davis choked out.

Cortez wasn't surprised that the gun fire had left him rattled. Even for a rookie, Davis was inexperienced with firearms. They looked as out of place in his hands as the controls of the drone looked in hers. The difference was, Cortez didn't need to be proficient in drone piloting to be a good agent. She placed what was meant to be a calming hand on his shoulder, but movement by the warehouse made her dig in her nails.

"We can't leave yet. We've got to buy our runner some time," she insisted, grateful Davis couldn't see her beating heart. She balled up her fists and dug her nails into her palms, leaving small crest shapes in the soft flesh.

Nina sprinted for the truck again. Moments after she exited the warehouse, the dog raced after her.

"Okay... okay... You know, I've always thought my fallback job would be 'fighter pilot," Davis said weakly.

Cortez had to smile. Even terrified, Davis tried to keep jokes coming.

"Alright top gun, keep those assholes distracted."

Davis bobbed and weaved, dipping lower over the guards to make sure he had their attention. The taller guard whipped out his handgun and joined his colleague in taking shots at the drone. Amidst the melee, a third figure appeared in the Mansion's doorway.

"There's our boy." Davis' voice went up a notch. "How ya doing, Mr. Savin."

Savin gestured to the drone, and even from 100 feet up in the air, the agents were able to hear him bellow, "Find out where it's coming from!"

"That's our cue to leave, right?" Davis eyed Cortez pleadingly.

Cortez watched the fuzzy shape of the beat up pickup truck exit the compound out the back.

"Yes. Bring her home." She said, nodding slowly. They had bought the runner a little time; she just hoped it had been enough.

Davis threw the drone forward, away from the mansion, just as the two guards jumped in their Jeep parked in front and immediately gave chase.

"I'm not sure I'm going to be able to land and collect the drone in time. They're right on my tail." Davis clenched the controls, his face and his knuckles stark white.

"Not to worry."

Cortez leapt from her seat at the desk and hopped behind the wheel.

"Let's take these boys for a ride."

Cortez punched the gas, nearly launching Davis out of his seat. Regaining his balance, Davis executed a series of tight maneuvers to get the drone off Savin's property and on the tail of the surveillance van.

"Alright... I got this. This is better than playing War Thunder."

"You're such a nerd." Cortex said lightly, her eyes focused on the task at hand but her heart slowed a little. She attempted a smile, but her lips would barely curl. Cortez kept her eye on Davis, along with the guards' jeep, in the rearview window. He was in the zone, bobbing and weaving, keeping pace with the van.

He might just make a hell of an agent yet, Cortez thought.

***

The room was greyed with morning light fighting its way through thick curtains. Savin sat on the edge of their bed. His bare shoulders trembled with rage. He had discovered the pillows carefully placed under the sheets where Nina should have been. He had shouted out for her, but he already knew she was gone. The elegance of the bedroom was Nina's doing. He gave her everything, and this was how she repaid him? Who did this bitch think she was? Savin swung his fist and smashed the table lamp to the ground sending glass flying. Then he ripped down the flowery curtains that she had picked out. Savin squinted and winced in pain as the bright sunlight fired into the room. He kicked down a bedside table as he marched out the door. It was Nina's fault the room was destroyed. It was Nina's fault that he would have to… handle her now.

His heart thrummed with the intensity of his anger. His hazel eyes dilated to almost completely black, as he aggressively pushed his normally slicked black-brown hair out of his eyes.

Perhaps if his life had taken a different turn things could have been different for him, but the man he had chosen to become was deadly. With every determined stride, he was seething with vengeance and pain.

He slid his phone out of the pocket of his grey sweatpants.

"Nina's gone. We need to find her." Savin felt lightheaded. It took everything in him not to scream.

The distracted voice of Harold, a somewhat portly man and one of Savin's trusted guards answered him. "Sir? But what about the drone?"

Just like that, Savin snapped. Harold wasn't the brightest bulb. But it was his stupidity that made him so damn infuriating.

"I don't give a *fuck* about the drone. Get back here *now*."

CHAPTER 3

— FRIEND OR FOE —

Nina eyed her furry companion warily. She had always liked animals; they just didn't seem to care for her. This one was no exception. The dog was asleep curled up on the edge of the passenger seat, right against the door, as far away from Nina as he possibly could be and still be in the truck. This at least made sense though, given how they had started off.

The dog could not have given her a harder time getting him out of the warehouse. If she got too close to him, he snapped at her, and not just in a warning way. If Nina had been within reach, she was quite certain he would not have hesitated to take a chunk out of her arm. So, Nina had untied him from the post instead of removing the loop of rope from his neck. Thinking the hard part was over, Nina began to jog from the barn, only to realize after a few steps that the dog had refused to follow her. Her pleas and cajoling had no effect on him. He simply stared at her with what could only be described as a skeptical look on his face. Nina was again reminded of her mother's old dog. When she was a child, he watched her play in a similar fashion, as though he wasn't quite sure what to make of her.

Nina had fully run out of ideas when the shots rang out. She instinctively hit the floor and the dog scampered into the corner and cowered. The panicked snarls, roars, and barks of the frightened animals filled the warehouse with a cacophony of sound. It took her a moment to realize the shots were not being directed at her.

"You need to go!" Nina begged the dog as she pushed herself up from the ground and began to jog towards the exit. He stared at her. More shots rang out.

"What are you waiting for? RUN!" she shrieked at the dog.

He didn't move.

Nina cautiously tugged on his rope, and whispered, "We *need*... to run, dog..."

Finally, finally, the dog rose from the corner and took off running for the open warehouse door. The pair sprinted across the lawn towards the pickup truck. Nina could hear the gunfire continuing to her left but did not risk turning to see who was shooting and who was being shot at. Leaping into the open door of the truck, Nina leaned across to open the passenger side. At the last second, she caught a glimpse of a bundle of fur flying through the air, right at the open passenger side window. Nina jerked back into her own seat as the dog came crashing down into his. The dog collected himself and sat up to face Nina. The two stared at each other, each feeling a mixture of confusion, adrenaline, and fear.

"Fine, well, I guess you're with me now," Nina remarked as she started the engine and took off toward the back exit of the compound.   The Dog braced himself up against the passenger door.

They cleared the compound and raced down the dirt road.   Nina's heart raced as she maneuvered the truck across the bumpy backroad.

"We just need to get to the main road and we will be ok..."

The Dog only huffed in response and pushed his face into the corner between the seat and the passenger window.

* **

Nina had taken so many twists and turns along her escape route that it had been an hour before she reached a paved road. Nina risked looking away from it to take a better look at the dog. He was a pitiful sight. Covered in deep gashes, fur caked in blood, it was a miracle he had been able to stand let alone run to the truck. The odor he emanated, that now filled every inch of the truck's cabin, provided further evidence of deep neglect and fear.

"Hey uh... are you okay? You don't smell very good... you don't look too good either."

The dog didn't move. Nina squinted. Was he still breathing? Dead asleep or nearly dead? Nina extended a slow, if shaky, hand toward the creature. Just before she made contact, the dog jerked awake, eyes wide and filled with aggression. Seeing Nina's outstretched hand, he lunged and flashed his teeth. Nina yanked her hand away and accidentally veered into the oncoming lane. Lucky for her, no other car had passed by them for miles.

"Hey!!! You almost BIT me!"

The dog pulled himself up into a sitting position. He seemed disoriented to Nina. She softened, realizing how terrified he must be. He didn't know Nina was trying to help, didn't realize they were on the path to freedom and not another fight. He was confused, scared as hell, and Nina couldn't blame him.

"You okay? Have a bad dream or something?"

The dog panted in reply. His bad breath rolled over Nina. That, on top of the fact that he already reeked, nearly made Nina gag. When she was able to meet his eyes again, all she saw was exhaustion.

"You need some water, don't you?"

Nina guided the car off to the side of the highway, right beside a sign reading 'Route 66 West' and unbuckled her seatbelt. Keeping her eyes on the dog, she slowly reached into the back seat for her backpack. Despite her caution, the dog raised its hackles and began a soft, low growl.

"Easy there, I'm not going to hurt you." Nina kept her voice low and sweet, knowing it would be awhile before the dog would even begin to trust her.

Nina pulled a wad of cash from her back pack and set it down on the edge of the dog's seat. He cocked his head and stopped growling for a moment as he took in the lump of hundred dollar bills. He sniffed it and began to tremble like a leaf, likely taking in Savin's scent.

With ginger care, Nina removed a bottle of water from her backpack. She took a deep swig for herself. She scanned the cab of the truck for something to pour it in for the dog but came up empty.

"Alright, this will have to do. Don't you bite me now."

Nina extended her hand to within reach of the dog and began to pour a few mouthfuls of water into it. Before she could draw the courage to move her hand closer to the dog, he darted forward and lapped the water straight from the bottle, splashing it across the car seat and onto the floorboards. Nina cringed as he slobbered onto the mouth of the bottle.

"Oh… ok… well, I guess this is your water bottle now."

Nina twisted the cap back onto the bottle and examined the damage. The dog had dribbled all over the seat, including over Savin's cash. Nina collected the cash with the tips of her fingers and tucked it into an outside pocket of the backpack.

"You're a sloppy drinker, you know that? You probably need some food, too, huh?" Nina threw the car back into drive. "And I could use something a little stronger to drink."

Nina could have sworn from the look in his eye that the dog was bemused by her statement.

Several miles down the road, Nina caught sight of a gas station. She left the car unlocked when she entered the store. The truck was the only car in the parking lot. When she glanced over her shoulder before entering the store, she was surprised to find the dog sitting up, alert with his face pressed against the passenger side window, watching her. He was in the same position when she exited the store and did not move until she opened the car door, at which point he resumed his seat as far away from Nina as possible. But when Nina set the brown grocery bag down on her seat, he couldn't help but sniff the air hopefully.

"Don't worry. I got you some real dog food. But we have to keep moving, so we're gonna share some beef jerky for now."

Nina extended a piece of jerky and the dog leaned forward to grab it without hesitation. His sudden movement made Nina jump and the jerky dropped onto the passenger seat. The dog ducked his head to scarf it up off the seat. Savin must have been starving him, she realized, and she felt a pang for the poor dog. The dog kept his head low to the seat as he chewed and Nina decided that now might be a good opportunity for them to try and bond. She extended a slow hand toward the top of the dog's head. Catching a glimpse of it in his peripheral vision, the dog let out a yelp. Nina yanked her hand back and the dog leapt away from her into the back seat of the truck, shaking again.

"I'm not going to hurt you. I promise."

Nina glanced down and realized the dog had left a chunk of the beef jerky behind. Pinching it between her thumb and index finger, she held it out to the dog. After a moment's hesitation, hunger won out and the dog tugged the small piece of jerky from her hand.

"See? I'm your friend. I rescued you, remember?"

The dog shot her a look and uttered a low growl in response.

"Fine. Grrrr to you too then." Nina huffed. She tore a bite out of her own beef jerky and peeled out of the gas station parking lot.

Back on the long barren road, Nina adjusted her rearview mirror to get a better look at the dog. He was panting and kept readjusting himself in the backseat.

"Hey bud, how about some music for the ride?" Nina flipped on the radio and scanned until she reached a country music station. Mellow guitar and soothing vocals came flowing from the speakers. Nina felt some of the tension leave her shoulders and she tapped the steering wheel in time with the music. When she looked up to check on the dog again, she saw he had curled up in the middle seat and fallen asleep.

Nina focused once again on the empty desert road in front of her. Where she was going, she wasn't sure.

***

Rock music came pounding out of the speakers in Savin's study. Harold and Carl did their best not to wince as they sat in their respective chairs in front of Savin's impressive oak desk. Savin paced behind his desk, unable to contain his anger enough to sit still.

"The bitch took my dog. Now there's some irony for ya," Savin spat. "Why the fuck did she do that?"

Neither Harold nor Carl possessed the courage, or the information, required to respond. So, they continued to sit in silence as their boss raged on. Savin paced from wall to wall again and slammed his fist down on the desk.

"How the hell did she get out of here?"

Harold cringed and cleared his throat. "Well, the uh... only vehicle missing is the truck we use for... transport and deliveries."

Savin froze. He turned to face Harold. In a flash, Savin was around the desk, grabbing Harold by the throat.

"Tell me the truck wasn't loaded," Savin said with as much forced calm as he could muster. Harold's eyes bugged out as he grasped at Savin's iron grip, making small choking noises in reply.

Carl leapt to answer in his place. "We... we were getting ready for a transport this morning–"

"Are you FUCKING kidding me?!"

Savin threw Harold back down in his seat and started to move toward Carl when a thought hit him. Moving back behind his desk, he whipped open the petty cash drawer to find it empty.

"She's not coming back."

"We'll find her," Harold coughed. He edged away from Savin, his hands rubbing his throat.

"No. I'll find her. And when I do, I'm going to kill her."

***

As Nina and the dog passed the 'Welcome to California' sign, Nina realized she had been driving for about nine hours. And she really had to pee again. The sun was dropping low in the sky and Nina decided they were far enough away from Savin to call it a day. The next rest stop they passed would be their home for the night.

"We're here. Wherever "here" is…" Nina called to the dog as the truck rolled to a halt in front of the dingy rest stop building. A man with a pot belly and round glasses waved to her as he passed the car. For a brief moment fear overwhelmed her. Did he recognize her? Did he think she looked out of place? Did he somehow know Savin and was on his way to call her ex-boyfriend now? The dog growled at the portly man as he passed the truck and Nina snapped out of it. She couldn't let fear get the better of her. They had a long way to go.

Nina scrambled from the truck and popped open the back door to let the dog out, but he just stared at her.

"Oh come on. I know you have to go too!" Nina groaned.

The dog panted at her and did not move.

"Come onnnn. You trusted me before, didn't you?" Nina tugged on the rope still dangling from the dog's neck. After a few seconds, the dog acquiesced and leapt from the car to Nina's great relief. Her relief was short lived as the dog took his sweet time relieving himself.

"Hey, can you hurry it up? I have to go too!"

Nina waddled toward the rest stop with the dog in tow. She swung open the door to the ladies' room and flew into the first stall, leaving the stall door slightly open to hold onto the dog's rope. As she went to sit down, the dog gave a great tug on the rope.

"Hey! Cut it out!"

The dog just let out a whining growl and tugged harder.

Stepping out of the stall, Nina massaged her arm and glared at the dog. He also seemed to be in a huff, standing with his back to her, nose in the air.

"You have no patience and no manners," Nina grumbled.

The dog uttered a half growl, half bark.

"Yeah, I'm talking to you. And you somehow smell worse now too."

The dog barked over his shoulder at her and tugged her towards the door.

Back at the truck, Nina tied the dog's rope to the tailgate and started to move to the front to grab her grocery bag. The dog moved to follow her.

"No, you stay. What am I saying? I bet you don't even know what that means." Nina shook her head. She grabbed the bag from the cab of the truck and returned to the truck bed to find the dog sitting, waiting obediently for her.

"Huh. Will wonders never cease..."

Nina plopped some dog food on a paper plate and set it down for the dog who began to gobble it down in huge bites. She opened a bag of chips, some crackers, and a container of cheese for herself. As the pair ate, Nina found her eyes drifting to the last item in her bag. There was a time when Nina would have turned her nose up at such a thing. It had claimed the lives of many of her friends and relatives. Nina laughed at herself. What was she now if not a dead woman walking? With that thought, she pulled the bottle of tequila from her bag and took a long, deep swig.

CHAPTER 4

— LAW AND RECKONING —

Agent Cortez cleared her throat. The noise sounded too loud in the silent briefing room full of colleagues waiting for her to continue. She knew they were not impressed. It was etched into every grimace, every furrowed brow, every set of glazed over, disinterested eyes. Most importantly, it was plainly evident on the face of Supervising Agent Sarah Stone. Her silver hair was slicked back in a tight bun that pulled her face into an expression of unflinching disdain. Cortez considered herself to be a courageous agent, a fearless public servant. But even she was a little afraid of Agent Stone.

Behind the projector in the back of the room, just a few feet in front of Stone, Davis tapped away at his computer. Cortez was glad Davis couldn't see their boss's face. It would have sent the already anxious agent into a tailspin. Cortez gestured for Davis to continue the visuals. Images of the exotic animals from the warehouse flashed across the screen. Some of the agents shifted in their seats, their attention piqued.

"As you can see, Savin has been trading in a number of exotic animals, all of which are illegal to own."

Images of the beaten dogs flashed across the screen. Davis paused the presentation on an image of the golden-brown shepherd dog. His piercing eyes seemed to look directly into the camera.

"He is holding them in the same warehouse he keeps his fighting dogs in. The animals have been gravely mistreated and abused—"

"Do you have any footage of the dog fights?" Stone interrupted.

"N-no. But it's pretty clear from the footage we do have that Savin is using the dogs in fights," Cortez stammered.

"That's circumstantial. You have no concrete evidence of the fights. Which is still the only thing we could arrest him for right now because you have even less evidence of the crimes you are supposed to be investigating, his multimillion-dollar drug and firearm dealings, and nothing on the network of criminals we are trying to bring down." Stone said crisply, folding her hands in front of her as though the issue was closed.

"We are working those angles, ma'am, but this obviously—"

"Need I remind you of the atrocities his drug dealing partner, Quintero has committed? Of all the reasons, bringing him down needs to be our top priority!"

"Yes, of course... All I'm saying is we know he is fighting these dogs! Quintero is important, I'm not refuting that, but so is *this*!"

Cortez gestured emphatically to the image of the bloodied and beaten shepherd mix dog. Somehow, the room seemed even quieter than before. Davis looked paler than normal. Cortez braced herself for a reprimand, but it did not come. Stone gazed up at the dogs and said nothing for a long moment.

"I understand, Cortez. I do. But there's not enough here. And we can't afford to lose Savin on a flimsy charge." Stone turned to go and the room began to disperse. "Come back to me when you have something solid. Actual photographic evidence, a witness, a wiretap—"

Cortez and Davis' eyes met.

"Wait!" Davis exclaimed, him and Cortez having the same brainstorm.

Stone turned back to find both agents on their feet. She paused, sure this would be a waste of time, as she took in the childlike grin on Davis's face.

"Bring up the footage," Cortez said.

Video of Nina climbing out the window played across the screen. Stone stepped forward, intrigued.

"This young woman was seen fleeing the mansion in an old pick-up truck early this morning. We believe she may be Savin's girlfriend. She took a couple bags and one of his dogs and didn't look back. If we could get her to talk… we'll have him," Cortez explained, relief flooding through her veins as she realized she may finally have what Stone was looking for.

"Have you ID'd her?" Stone asked.

"Uhhhh…" Cortez looked desperately at Davis. He had submitted the woman's photo to facial recognition while they were in route back to the office. She watched the young agent type frantically as he pulled up the database on his computer.

"YES!" Davis shouted, causing the remaining agents in the room to spin around and glare at him.

"I mean… yes. Her name is Nina Locklear, a twenty-two-year-old Native American woman from the Navajo Reservation just north of Tucumcari, New Mexico."

Stone nodded, eyebrow raised. "Did you get a picture of the license plate?"

"Yes."

"Good. Find her."

***

Savin watched the jeep roll up the front drive through a window in the foyer. Harold parked it in its regular spot, about twenty yards from the front of the mansion. The engine quieted, but neither Harold nor Carl exited the vehicle. Savin felt a rush of heat fill his face. The men were dawdling. They did not have good news.

When the two men finally walked through the front door, they were greeted by Savin standing in the middle of the foyer with his arms crossed. He pointed to his study and the men headed straight in without a word.

"Well? What did you find out?" His voice was the kind of quiet that meant he was beyond angry. The calm before the storm, so to speak. Harold and Carl had their eyes trained on the floor, too scared to look up.

Harold and Carl exchanged glances. "We went to the reservation…" Carl began.

"She wasn't there. We roughed up some res-rats pretty good though," Harold finished. He attempted a smile that wasn't reciprocated.

Savin seethed in silence at his two henchmen. Unable to stand the silence and Savin's withering gaze, Carl continued.

"I think she's somewhere else."

"You think… she's somewhere… else. Now that's some quick thinking for ya!" Savin roared in disgust. He grabbed a long, thin letter opener off his desk and flung it at Carl's head. Carl ducked in just the nick of time.

"What more do I have to do to spell this out for you two idiots?" Savin bellowed. "If we don't get that truck back…"

Savin swallowed hard.

"He'll kill us all."

***

The stars spun wide, arching circles above her as Nina spun to the beat of the country music cranking from her radio. The tequila sloshed around the half empty bottle. She felt her heart beating in her ears. The sound of it reminded her of the drums her family played during blessingway rituals. Without her noticing, her wild dancing morphed into something that almost resembled the sacred movements she used to know by heart. The sounds of her tribe's chanting echoed in her mind. She was once again at home on her reservation. The memory of her Kinnalda ceremony flooded in. Her coming of age into womanhood. Her mother had gently combed her hair and braided it. She was dressed in a traditional Changing Woman's rug dress and Navajo blanket. In the 4-day ceremony, she was to be "molded" from a girl into a woman by her mother. Her family and the medicine men and women sang songs and prayed.

On the first day, she was given her spiritual connection. The second day she learned about the emotions of being a woman. The third and fourth day, she learned what is required to take care of your family. These memories buried deep in her heart, rumbled like distant thunder. "Take care of your family." She spoke outload as if from a dream.

This was the Navajo way. And she had thrown it all away.

The realization of what she was doing brought her to a crashing halt. She scanned the empty parking lot for the umpteenth time but saw no witnesses to her moment of longing and nostalgia. Except for the dog. He kept his careful eyes trained on her, full of apprehension.

"You know wwwwhat, dog?" Nina slurred. "They may dress me up... cover me in jewels when they feel like it..."

She slurped some more tequila.

"But I'm still no one. And... It... Just... doesn't matter"

Nina found herself facing the long stretch of empty road they would be traveling the next morning. She sucked in a breath and turned her face to the sky.

"We don't matter to ANYONE. WE ARE NOTHING!"

The wild dancing and ranting and drinking were no longer enough to alleviate her pain. Nina raised the tequila bottle over her head and brought it swinging back down to earth with a mighty crash. Nina watched the shards of glass dance across the pavement, right up to the feet of the dog, who sat cowering where he was tied by the truck bed. Nina saw nothing but fear in his eyes.

"Oh no… No I'm sorry… Please… I think I just need to sleep…"

Nina tried to approach the dog, but he leapt up into the truck bed and whine-growled at her. Tears filled her eyes.

"I'm so sorry…"

***

Nina jerked awake to the sound of rapping on her window. Through her throbbing headache, Nina gathered the wherewithal to check and make sure she got the dog in the car before she passed out. To her great relief he was standing in the back seat on full alert, staring at Nina's fogged up window. Nina's heart leapt into her throat as she registered a figure standing on the other side of the clouded glass. The figure tapped the window again and the dog barked loudly.

"Highway Patrol. Roll down your window."

Nina sucked in a shaky breath. The dog growled louder as Nina followed the officer's command and lowered her window. The early morning sunlight filtering in over the man's shoulder made Nina wince.

"Ahh… yes, officer?"

A mustached police officer with dark sunglasses and a cowboy hat peered down at Nina. He leaned into the car and gave the truck's cab a careful scan. The dog growled again and raised his hackles. The officer put one hand on his gun.

"This isn't a campground. You can't stay here overnight." He kept his hand on the gun but took a step back from the truck, indicating he would flee before he'd shoot.

"Yes sir. I'm on my way now."

The police officer lowered his sunglasses and scanned the cab again. Nina held her breath.

"Ok. Get a move on. You have a nice day now."

The officer walked slowly back towards his vehicle. Nina turned the engine and guided the car out of the parking lot. She gave the officer a wave and a forced smile as she went by, but he was no longer looking at her. He was squinting down at the laptop on his dashboard. Nina could hear the dog whining from the back seat. She glanced into her rearview mirror and saw him panting and pacing in frantic circles.

"It's ok. We're ok…"

Their eyes met in the rearview mirror. She could have sworn he understood her. Either way, the dog stopped spinning and sat down as they set off back onto the long empty road.

CHAPTER 5

— TRUTH AND JUSTICE —

Davis hustled down the hallway, skirting around other agents and the errant civilian in his path. Of course, she wasn't at her desk. Cortez hated to be cooped up for any lengthy period of time. At Cortez's request, Davis had put an APB out on both Nina and the truck. Just a couple hours after facial recognition identified Nina Locklear, the APB turned up a report from a highway patrol officer and a notification from the DMV identifying the owner of the truck as Eduardo Hernandez. It took a moment for Davis to register the name, but once it clicked, he took off running.

His mad dash to Cortez's office earned him some laughs and funny looks, but nothing he wasn't used to. He was still the new, untested rookie. Green about the ears, and just about everywhere else judging by the way most of the other agents treated him. Though Cortez, his partner and mentor, granted him the most respect out of anyone in the office by far, Davis knew that even she did not consider him a full agent in his own right. This thought added a zing to Davis' step that propelled him around the corner and into the bullpen.

Cortez stood chatting with the rather large and muscular Agent Cairns by the edge of the sea of desks and cubicles. He gave Davis a bemused smile as he screeched to a halt by Cortez' side. Cairns smirked.

"What have you got, Davis?" Cortez asked, giving Davis a moment to catch his breath.

"Eduardo… Hernandez…" Davis blurted out.

That wiped the smirk off Cairn's face. "You don't mean–"

"Aka Eduardo Quintero." Cortez interjected. "Could you excuse us, Cairns?"

Without waiting for a response, Cortez grabbed Davis by the elbow and dragged him into an alcove off of the bullpen. Davis could see Cairns sulking over Cortez's shoulder.

"Speak," she demanded.

"DMV came through… ID'd the truck as belonging to Quintero. Do you think this means that… Nina Locklear works for him?"

"For her sake, I certainly hope not. If we can get her testimony on top of the footage of the truck on Savin's property, that establishes a clear link between him and Quintero. Did we get anything on the truck's location?" Cortez clicked her pen rapidly, thinking.

"A report came in this morning from a highway patrolman stating that he stopped a woman matching Nina's description in a truck with New Mexico plates at the Nevada/California border. He also reported an extremely "aggressive" dog in the back seat."

Cortez's eyes flashed with excitement as she whipped out her cellphone.

"Who are you call—" Davis started but Cortez waved her arm to shush him.

"Shh… Supervisor Stone, we have her headed across the border into California… No, ma'am I'd like to go out there myself… Yes, ma'am I'll be taking Davis with me," she said into the phone and winked at Davis.

Davis raised his hands and shook his head hard, but Cortez just waved him off.

"Of course, We'll report back when we know more. Thank you."

Cortez slipped her phone in her pocket, grabbed Davis by the arm and tugged him down the hall.

"Grab your go bag, Davis. We've got a witness to find."

"Um, I'm really more of a tech guy. Not a 'boots on the ground guy'."

Cortez rolled her eyes. "Come on, it'll be fun. Like your… War… Warriors. That computer game you like so much."

"You mean War Thunder."

"Oh, is that what the cool kids are calling it?"

Davis laughed, but it sounded thin and high to him. He hoped Cortez didn't notice.

"Are you sure you don't want to go with someone a little bit more… more like him?" Davis gestured to Cairns as they passed his desk. Cairns saw him point and scowled.

"I know scarecrows with more brains than Cairns. I'll see you at my car in ten. I'm driving."

CHAPTER 6

—— THE BAD-MAN ——

The warm sea air wrapped around Nina in swaths. For the first time in recent memory Nina could say she felt almost relaxed. She slipped her shoes off, scooped them up in one hand, and stepped out into the cool beach sand, still damp from last night's high tide. For a moment, she forgot herself, where she was, and what she was doing.

She sighed as she contemplated the sand between her toes. Something felt oddly familiar to her, yet in truth, it was unlike anything she had ever seen, or felt before. It was different from the hot dry desert sand from where she was born. The Navajo Nation's poorest reservation. Well, they called it a "reservation", but for her, it had felt like prison. She loved her family. She loved her indigenous roots. God she loved it. She was proud of that part. But on the reservation, there was no running water. Often no electricity. The rest of the world was living and thriving, but for Nina, and her tribe, everything started to seem unobtainable. Savin's dangerously handsome good looks, and endless supply of drugs and alcohol filled her needs with ease. And then there was his money. Lots of it. Drug money.

She wasn't proud of herself, and the way things had turned out. Her face cringed at the memory of it all. Any chance she could to find a better life for herself, she would take it. It was the only way to survive. Drugs and alcohol temporarily sheltered her from pain, only to have it reappear in the morning with even more tenacity.

An uncertain whimper at her side brought her back to the here and now. She looked down to find the dog gazing with apprehension at the gentle waves dropping against the shore. She sat down in the sand next to him. Not too close... but as near to him as she felt he would find comfortable.

"Bet you've never seen anything like that before, huh?" Nina smiled. "Neither have I. Not in person, anyways... Just in pictures."

The two absorbed the moment.

Nina glanced at her backpack laying in the sand next to her. She picked it up and opened up one of the side pockets and pulled out a cell phone. She knew there was a chance she could be tracked. She decided to take the risk. She turned it on. There were dozens of voice mail messages. Most of the messages were from James Savin... but one was from her mom. She tapped it, and her mother's voicemail played out on the speaker.

"Nina?... Nina... Honey... Please be safe.... Don't come home now... They were here looking for you..."

The dog's ears perked up as he listened as well.

Nina's mother finished in her native Navajo "Just stay safe, my child... I love you."

Nina took a deep inhale. The dog watched her closely

and let out a slight whine as Nina's breathing turned into choked back tears. He didn't know what was happening but somehow he knew it wasn't good.

Nina looked down at her phone again and reluctantly hit play on the screen where it read: Voicemail – James Savin.

Savin's voice came rocketing through.

"You BITCH! You are NOTHING without me! Go back to your damn reservation, live in poverty and fucking ROT!"

The dog jumped, his hackles raised up high on his back. He looked all around to see where that voice was coming from. Nina quickly grabbed the end of his rope as he pulled back in fear.

Nina tried to comfort the dog, "It's ok… he's not here… it's just the…"

She dropped the phone while trying to hang on to the dog. Savin's enraged voice played on.

"You better hope that I never find you, because when I do, I'm gonna kill YOU!!!!"

The dog growled and whined in fear of the voice he heard. Savin's voice. The "badman" that brings pain.

"Do you hear me Nina… you are a NOTHING WORTHLESS… PIECE OF…"

Nina quickly dug the phone from the sand and smacked her finger down on it to delete the message, stopping Savin's hateful, murderous rant.

The dog let out a slight whimper as he scanned all around him.

"He's not here. I promise." Nina tried to comfort him.

Nina could almost see his heart beating through his thick fur.

"He isn't going to find us. Don't worry... It will be ok." Nina told the dog. She attempted to convince herself that was true as well.

Nina and the dog sat silently together for a while regaining their composure. The soothing sound of the ocean waves helped them escape, at least for today, from those terrible thoughts of the *bad-man*.

"I have an idea." Nina softly whispered to the dog.

His head tilted as he tried to discern her whisper.

She lightly tugged the dog's rope and guided him closer to the gentle breaking waves at the shoreline. He followed with a moderate amount of hesitation. Midway down to the shore, Nina set her backpack and shoes on the sand. No need to get them wet. Nina stepped into the waves first. The dog watched as the water curled around Nina's ankles and swept back out to sea. Nina bent over and scooped up some water with her free hand, tossing it in the direction of the dog. The water splashed onto the sand next to the dog. The dog pounced on the spot where it landed in a playful manner. Nina repeated the game a little closer to the water's edge. In no time the dog gleefully had joined her in the sea.

Nina and the dog felt free. The ocean seemed to almost have a healing power. The two frolicked through the shallow water, dipping under, rolling through the seafoam. Nina laughed at the murky clouds he left in his wake.

"Well, this is one way to get you clean."

As if in response, the dog gave a mighty shake, covering Nina in ocean spray.

Nina danced back and laughed. "Fair enough. I probably don't smell great either."

The two frolicked and played along the shoreline for quite a while. It seemed to Nina that the ocean had some kind of power to bring out the "play" in both of them. It cleansed them a little on the outside and a little on the inside. Some of the dried blood on the dog's legs and face washed away. At least for today, Nina's "grrrr-dog" seemed almost like a puppy again.

A low flying seagull darted by the pair, back up towards the sand and down the beach. The dog's eyes lit up. With one sharp tug, the tattered rope fell away from his neck, and he was off running down the beach after the seagull!

"Hey, wait, no! Where are you going?!" Nina cried out. "No, no, no this isn't happening!"

She charged out of the waves after the bird and dog, but it was no use. Both animals seemed to fly across the sand, and she was left far behind in their wake. She ran until she lost sight of the dog around a bend and then collapsed to the sand. Silent tears rolled down her face. For a moment, Nina could barely breathe. Finally, she spoke, berating herself.

"I suppose you're better off without me... I can't do anything right..."

Nina rose and headed back up the beach, leaving the tattered rope discarded behind her. She returned to her backpack sitting alone and unguarded in the sand. She opened it up, and touched the cash. It was all still there...

and then she closed her eyes in sadness. She pulled out her cell phone once again.

Nina dialed a number with shaky fingers. After five rings, an old woman's voice finally answered on the other end.

"Hello? Nina?"

"Mom, it's me…"

"Nina! Are you ok?"

"Yes. Mom, I'm so sorry… Did they hurt you??"

There was a moment of silence on the end of the line. Nina closed her eyes.

"No," her mom said finally, her voice trembling. "They just tried to frighten us. But you can't come back here. They're looking for you. They say you stole a car?"

"I *took* a truck to get away." Nina said firmly.

She could hear her mom stifling a sob. "Where are you going? What are you going to do?"

Nina didn't know and she admitted so.

"Mom, I'm so sorry…. He pretended to be someone different when I met him. I should never have… I feel so ashamed."

"You were trying to make a better life for yourself. This is not a life for you here. He came here buying up everything. Throwing his money around… making promises… but then the drugs… and now…"

Nina's mom continued in a whisper, choked with tears.

"He sent his men here to tell me he is going to kill you…"

Nina tried to console her, although her own voice was shaking. "I *will* be ok. I will think of something. He will never hurt us again."

"I love you, Nina. Stay safe, my daughter."

"I love you too, Mom."

Nina let the phone tumble from her limp hand back into the sand. For a moment, the weight of her situation was overwhelming, suffocating. She felt her senses dulled by fear induced helplessness. Pure desperation overtaking her, Nina scooped up the phone and sprinted to the edge of the water. With all her might, she flung the phone out into the sea. She lied down in the sand and cried.

CHAPTER 7

CHANCE OR CIRCUMSTANCE

Nina wasn't sure how much time had passed, but the sensation of something cold and wet against her hand brought her back to her body. Nina shivered and opened her eyes to see the dog staring at her with his golden brown, concerned eyes. Nina had no time to process his return before a voice interrupted them.

"Is he your dog?"

Nina turned to find a half-dressed man, surfboard tucked under his arm, standing about fifteen feet away, watching her. He had a shy smile that complimented his gentle, crystal blue eyes, sun bleached surfer hair and muscular shoulders. The rolled down wetsuit he wore exposed his browned skin and defined abs. Nina found herself speechless as he spoke.

"Um, I found him at the south end of the beach. He followed me back here. I thought he might be lost."

Nina nodded and just stared.

The dog studied them both, cocking his head from side to side.

"I'm Charlie, by the way."

"Hi… yes… thank you."

"It's funny; I thought your dog was following me, but I guess he was coming back to you." Charlie gave her a good-natured smile. "I live just up that hill. The surf shop."

Charlie pointed to a cute bungalow and surf shop, a ways up from the beach. Private and idyllic. Turning back to Nina, Charlie's brow crinkled.

"You've, uh, you've actually got a bit of sand on your face."

Nina was mortified to realize that a big patch of sand was stuck on her face. She clumsily tried to wipe it off with her shirt sleeve.

"Um, right, thank you. And thanks for… um… walking with my dog," she said, flustered.

"No problem. I'll be going then." Charlie took a couple steps toward his house then stopped. He turned back to Nina, blushing.

"Hey, do you, uh, live near here?"

"No, I'm just passing through."

"Right, right, well, have a nice night!" Charlie gave Nina and her dog a sweet smile. "Later pup!" He spoke right to the dog.

The dog's tail wagged in response.

Nina smiled at Charlie's retreating back. The dog gave a soft woof in Charlie's direction, as if to call him back, but

Charlie continued up the beach. Nina crouched by the dog's side so that they were eye to eye. The dog looked from Nina to Charlie and back again. His consternation was clear. Nina laughed.

"Aren't you a funny one?"

Ever so slowly, Nina extended her hand toward the dog. The dog accepted her touch without flinching and she gently patted his fur with her fingertips.

"Thank you for coming back."

The dog gave her a whining woof in reply.

"I think you need a name… How about… Nitch'i Aki? I can call you Aki for short. What do you think?"

Aki woofed. Nina took that as his stamp of approval.

***

Nina shot up in her bed with a shriek, grasping her throat with both hands, struggling to breath. For a moment, she had no idea where she was. Then hazy memories of checking into a Motel-6 before passing out came drifting back to her. A soft thump on the bed let her know Aki had awoken as well. Within seconds she could feel his hot breath on her face. He gave her a couple licks until she laughed and pushed him away. The images of the dog fights that plagued her dreams were receding, but she could still feel Savin's hands on her throat. Swallowing her residual fear, Nina put on a small smile and turned to Aki.

"So, are we good now, you and I? Friends?"

Aki moved closer and set his head down on her lap. Nina glanced at his half of the bed and realized it was covered in sand.

"Man, you need a bath."

Aki's ears shot back at the word and he hurried to hop off the bed.

"Haha. I guess you know that word."

Aki whined at the second mention of 'bath,' but when Nina rose and headed for the bathroom, he followed with some intense coaxing, and his tail hanging low and his ears down.

Aki talked back. "Grrrr...."

"Ok, Grrrr-dog. You smell and we have to get you in the bathtub!"

Aki didn't try to bite Nina, but he definitely played a fun game of "catch-me-if-you-can".

It took Nina two hours to fully clean Aki. Half the battle was getting through Aki's matted fur. The other half was keeping him in the tub. Aki squirmed and splashed and took every opportunity he saw to leap out of the tub. By the time Nina had finished cleaning him, the entire bathroom was a mess of mud, fur, and water. But at least he was clean! Nina opened the bathroom door and Aki shot out into the bedroom. He jumped all over the hotel room, from the floor to the bed, trying to get that darn "clean" smell off.

"Aki... No... not on the bed!"

Nina couldn't help but laugh. Aki finally jumped down onto the carpeted floor.

"You have to admit you feel better now."

Aki just barked.

Nina moved next to Aki. She attempted to finish off his grooming with a nice towel dry and a bit of brushing. She used the only brush she had. Her own. His fur fluffed into the air like giant snow-flakes.

As she gently brushed him, she discovered the puncture wounds from the dog fight, still in need of healing, as well as old scars that had left permanent marks on his legs. Nina whispered to him.

"I'm so sorry..."

Aki's golden brown eyes stared up at her. They seemed to silently speak volumes.

"No one will hurt us again."

Aki crawled a little closer.

"I bet you were a really cute puppy. How could anyone have ever given you away?"

They were silent for a moment as she gently stroked his fur.

Finally, Nina stood up and caught a glance at herself in a mirror hanging across the room. The sight of her reflection made her gasp. She was covered in soapy, dirty, doggy water, and fur.

"My turn!"

Aki gave her a head tilt.

After her turn in the shower and feeling cleaned up herself, Nina gathered her backpack and turned to the now semi-dry Aki.

"You hungry boy? Because I'm pretty hungry."

Aki jumped up and down, barking excitedly. Nina smiled and swung the door open, nearly walking straight into the housekeeper. Nina froze. She hadn't intended for anyone to see her at the motel, or the mess of fur behind her.

"I'm here for housekeeping," the woman said in a thick European accent.

Nina nudged Aki out the door, taking care to block the maid from getting a good look inside. The maid gave her a confused look.

"Are you ready for housekeeping this morning?"

"Uhhh…"

Nina grabbed a chunk of cash from her backpack and handed it to the maid.

"Our little secret, okay? And… sorry for…" Nina gestured to the half-closed door and hurried off down the hall with Aki, leaving the stunned maid in the hallway gazing in awe at the money. As they rounded the corner, the maid's cry of shock and dismay echoed after them.

"Sorry!" Nina yelled again and grinned at Aki as they took off running. She knew he smiled back.

CHAPTER 8

THE CHASE

"I hope whoever you sold the drugs and truck to, gave you a good price. It has to be at least equal to how much you value your life."

Eduardo Quintero leaned over Savin's oak desk, his nicotine-stained breath curling Savin's nose hairs. If Savin didn't know how serious the man was, Quintero's presence might have seemed cartoonishly overdone. The chains, the wife beater, the ever present Uzi, Savin had eyed in the back of Quintero's Black Hummer... it was like something out of a movie. But staring into Quintero's eyes, Savin knew the threat was all too real.

"I didn't sell the truck. My... ex... girlfriend stole it from me."

"Right. And I'm supposed to believe that you just left millions of dollars' worth of cash and drugs so unprotected that your two-bit whore was able to walk off with it. Tell me now, who are you working with? Tell me the truth and this next part might not hurt so much."

Quintero un-holstered the pistol strapped to his side and held the barrel to Savin's forehead. Savin could feel beads of sweat racing down his cheeks.

"No, no! I'm telling you the truth! The bitch stole the truck and took off with it!"

"You LOST my TRUCK?!"

"No!!! She... stole... it..."

Savin's breathing was tight and thin. The purity of the rage in Quintero's eyes was like nothing he had ever seen.

"You IDIOT." Quintero spun away from Savin, ranting in Spanish.

"Wait, slow down. I can't understand you."

"There's a tracking device on the truck. That's why I was giving you the chance to come clean. I would have found it anyway. If you had told me it had been stolen when it happened, we could have started following it DAYS ago!"

"Tell me where the truck is and I'll retrieve it right now." Savin asked.

"Oh no. I'm going with you. Can't trust you with this on your own apparently."

"Alright... but when we find the truck, the girl is mine."

"HA. You will have the girl if, and only if, I get my truck back with everything in it."

Savin gave a grudging nod. Quintero took out his phone and opened an app.

"She's in California."

***

"We've got a hit!"

Cortez grinned as Davis gave himself a silent fist pump. His nerves seemed to be fading already.

"Looks like she used her cell phone yesterday in Ventura County."

"Great job, Davis. Where was she exactly?"

"Well, I can only narrow it down to a region based off the cell phone tower ping, but it gives us a place to start."

"We'll head over there and start digging around. Maybe a local has seen something."

Cortez saw Davis fidgeting with his laptop out of the corner of her eye. After a moment, he continued.

"The Los Angeles field office sent us a message as well."

"Excellent. Do they have more intel on Quintero?"

"They have reliable intel placing Quintero on a plane that touched down in New Mexico yesterday. Reports are that he headed there to meet with Savin."

Cortez sighed and gripped the steering wheel tightly. "I wonder if Ms. Locklear knows she is running for her life."

CHAPTER 9

— SPIRIT FRIEND —

Charlie, along with a number of skilled Ventura beach surfers were taking advantage of the best waves of the day. Charlie was the most skilled in the bunch, Nina had decided. Not that she was any kind of expert, she bemused herself. But he sure looked like he knew what he was doing.

He seemed to always be in just the right spot. A large wave almost appeared to come to him. Skillfully, he turned his board and took a few powerful strokes and jumped to his feet in a smooth motion before flying down the wall of the wave. His graceful movements seemed second nature.

She sat with Aki, sharing a cheap fast food meal, while enjoying the sites. She casually glanced around the beach. She didn't intend for Charlie to notice her there. But next thing she knew, he was paddling to shore right towards her. He stepped out onto the sand with his bronze skin glistening, surfboard under his arm, shaking his wet hair out, striding directly over to her.

Nina took a deep breath in, as her heart raced, full of uncertainty. What the hell was she doing sitting on the beach, watching some *surfer*? She should be miles away by now. But where would she go? She pondered that question, as she watched Charlie coming closer.

"I thought you were just passing through?" he asked as he approached.

Nina set her hardly touched fast food burger back down on the bag it came in and turned to smile at him as casually as possible. Aki, who had been engrossed in his own soggy lunch, popped up at the sound of Charlie's voice and wagged his tail.

"I… ah… I thought I might stay a while." Nina hoped Charlie would blame her red cheeks on the sun.

"Well, I'd ask you to lunch, but it looks like you've already eaten. It's a shame because I make the BEST huevo rancheros…" Charlie grinned.

Nina glanced at the sad burger before her then over to Aki, who had polished off the rest of his before Charlie could finish his sentence. He stuck his nose in Nina's bag and before either of them could grab him he emerged with Nina's burger hanging out of his mouth. They both laughed at his antics.

"… I mean, I think Aki is still pretty hungry…" Nina said after the laughter had subsided.

Charlie's grin widened. Nina's stomach growled and she felt the blush in her cheeks darken further.

"…and I think I could have a bite or two."

Charlie gave her that incredible smile of his, and extended his hand to pull her to her feet.

Nina's breathing halted for a moment, as the warmth of his hand wrapped around hers. Nina desperately tried to shake it off as her imagination. But even after his hand released her. She felt a fire.

That doesn't happen. She told herself silently in her mind. *At least not to me. Not ever.*

One thing Nina knew for *certain*… She would *never* again be that gullible little native girl from the reservation. She must keep her wits about her.

Charlie, Nina and Aki walked toward Charlie's beach house, passing the old truck Nina took to get away. The truck almost seemed to watch them as they passed. The tracking device that was hidden inside it, was like a ticking time bomb of trouble.

***

Nina felt at ease in Charlie's home for reasons she could not explain. It wasn't her style by any means (surfer chic with a side of bohemian), but as she wandered through his living room examining the surfing trophies that decorated tabletops and bookcases, this stranger's living room felt like home to her. She couldn't help but to slightly relax her guard.

"Would you like a beer?" Charlie called from the kitchen, which looked into the living room. The smell emanating from the pan in front of Charlie was nothing short of heavenly. "...or maybe a mimosa?"

"Um... No, thank you. I'm all set." Nina tried to push the temptation of alcohol away from her brain. All it would do is cloud her judgement, make her susceptible.

"Well, that's good. I don't actually have the ingredients to make a mimosa."

Nina stifled her laugh. She scooped up a photo of Charlie and a few other surfers smiling on the beach of a coast with a lush jungle. She gently ran her fingers over glittering trophies and bold medals, all proudly on display. She noticed most of them were gold and silver. "Did you win all of these?"

Charlie turned toward a set of plates on the counter with his steaming pan of eggs and began to dole them out. "Yep."

"That's amazing!"

"It was. Until I tore my ACL in Bali. That was the end of competing for me."

"Oh... I'm so sorry."

"Nah, don't be! Sometimes something really great can come out of something bad." Charlie flashed her that grin again and Nina felt her heart skip a beat.

"Here we go! My famous huevo rancheros!"

Charlie set two plates of eggs down on his kitchen table. Hearing the scrape of ceramic on wood, Aki raced to Charlie's side and let out several resounding 'woofs.'

"Aki! Be polite! I'm sorry..." Nina turned to Charlie sheepishly.

"Hey, he knows what he wants." Charlie replied as he set eggs down in a bowl for Aki. "So, his name is Aki?"

Charlie glanced at Aki's nicks, and old scars that were still all too apparent within his coat.

"Uh, yeah. It's short for Nitch'i Aki's. It means *spirit friend*. He's a, uh, rescue."

Nina scooped a big bite of eggs into her mouth and closed her eyes to stop them from rolling back. The eggs were just that good. When she opened them again, she realized Charlie was not eating. He was sitting with his fork hovering over his plate, staring at her. Nina put a hand over her mouth to cover her zealous chewing.

"What?"

"You never actually told me your name."

Nina froze for a beat and pretended she needed to sneeze (she was an excellent fake sneezer, a skill that came in handy for times like this). It gave her time to recover and decide what she wanted to say. When her eyes met Charlie's again the lie fell effortlessly from her lips.

"Katera."

Nina cringed but held a smile. It was better he didn't know who she was. She would be moving on soon enough anyways.

"Tell me about yourself, Katera." Charlie seemed to realize he had been staring. His fork dove into the eggs and made a quick exit into his mouth.

"Not much to tell."

"I doubt that."

Nina held her breath. He was gazing at her again. She could feel his sincerity, and she was feeling something as well. She could not take her eyes away.

"I'm from New Mexico... I grew up on a Navajo Reservation."

"Oh wow, really? That must have been..."

"Hard? Yes, but sometimes something great can come out of something bad." Nina gave him a gentle smile.

Charlie smiled back with that happy grin of his, and his soft gentle eyes held on to hers for a moment. "Yes. Sometimes it does." That smile could light the darkest night. Nina cautioned herself. Too many emotions flowing through her mind.

***

The surf shop smelled of chemicals, saw dust, and dried seaweed. Nina was surprised to find she liked it. Dozens of surfboards hung from the walls. Each one was designed differently Nina realized. Different shapes, lengths, materials, paint patterns. Charlie took her by the hand and pulled her through the doorway, deeper into the shop.

"Did you make all of these?" Nina asked in awe.

"Well, most of them. Each board is designed for a particular person and the waves that they like to surf. This one is good for easy turns, this one is good for tricks…"

"How about this one?" Nina touched her fingertips to a short, light green, rounded board with two thin white stripes down the middle. Charlie nodded approvingly.

"That's an Egg. She's a 5'6" round tail. Good for beginners if you ever want to give it a try." He wiggled his eyebrows at her and Nina felt fire come to her cheeks. She turned quickly, admiring another board.

"You really do like eggs, don't you?" Nina joked to change the subject. On the far side of the workshop, she spotted a dark all-wood board on display. "And what about that one? What's his story?"

Charlie gestured for Nina to join him by the board.

"This one is very special," Charlie remarked. Nina could see an extra gleam in his eyes as he looked at the board.

"It's been all around the world. It's like an old soul; it's lived a thousand lives. It's all wood, made by my mentor in the style surfboards were made one hundred years ago. It's an amazing feeling to surf one of these. I've always wanted to catch the proverbial 'best wave ever' on one of these. They can handle huge waves. A great surfboard... pulling into a stellar wave..."

Charlie begins to act out his fantasy, adopting his surfing stance and extending his arms.

"...riding into the tube... letting it curl up around you... 'course you can't wait too long or it'll swallow you up... But when it all comes together at just the right moment... It's amazing. There's nothing else quite like it."

"You make it sound amazing." She gently smiled at him.

The pairs' eyes met. Charlie took a step toward Nina. She could have sworn he was about to say something else, but at the last second pivoted to—

"Erm, soooo, check this out!"

Charlie flung open the back door of the shop to reveal a room filled with power tools and a long table. On the table, Nina saw an unfinished board that looked remarkably like Charlie's mentor's. Charlie stepped up to the board and Nina followed suit.

"I'm building this all-wood board from scratch, like my mentor did. I have it shaped pretty well, every little bump needs to be worked out for it to ride smoothly. It takes time."

Charlie took Nina's hand and placed it against the board. She felt frozen in time with his touch. He ever-so-softly guided her hand.

"Feel this?"

With his hand on top of Nina's, Charlie gently slid her fingers along the edge of the board. At the end of the board, Charlie guided her fingers to the other side and slid them back along.

"See? It isn't the same as the other side. It's going to pull right" Charlie continued moving her hand across the board, his fingers ever so softly caressing the tops of hers.

As if he was truly envisioning the board streaming through the wave, Charlie continued. His touch was kind and gentle. She looked up at his face, as their intertwined fingers moved up the side of the board. His eyes connected with hers. Together, their fingers moved over an unbalanced, slightly rough patch of the board once again.

"Can you feel it?" He held his gaze.

It was just an innocent moment, she thought to herself. Yet, the attraction was undeniable. As close as he was to her, she wondered if he could feel her heart race.

"Yes, I... I can..." Her breathing was so tight; she could barely speak.

Nina took a deep breath in, as her mind tried to take back control.

Nina leapt back. For a moment, she had felt herself sinking, drifting off into... something. She needed to be alert. She needed to get out of there.

"I think I should go now." Nina sputtered.

"I'm sorry, is everything—?"

"Thank you for the food. Your surfboards are great. I'm just going to collect my dog and get out of your hair. You probably need to get back to work. Goodbye now!"

"Katera, is everything ok? I didn't mean to…"

***

As Nina turned the truck out of the parking lot, she heard an odd little rumbling noise from Aki. When she turned to look at him, he refused to turn, instead staring ahead in silence. When Nina looked back to the road, Aki gave her another little huffing growl.

"What?"

This time Aki turned to meet her gaze with a rather cross expression.

"Grrrr…. hhhhhrrrumpph."

"No. It's a bad idea."

"Grrrrr… RUFF."

"I said NO. It's too dangerous!"

Aki let out a snort that sprayed Nina with a fine mist of snot. She flicked a droplet away from her eye with her index finger.

"Your objections have been duly noted."

CHAPTER 10

—— THUNDER ROLLS ——

Until meeting Aki, Nina had had no idea that dogs could hold grudges. But here was Aki, insisting on taking up half the motel bed and sleeping with his back to her. He was somehow hogging all the blankets too, which was a remarkable feat for a creature without opposable thumbs. Aki had made it quite clear that he was mad at her and was delivering his own dog-version of the 'silent treatment.' Though that didn't stop him from adding periodic commentary in the form of whines and growls.

"You're taking over the WHOLE bed!"

"Grrrrrrrrrumph."

"Oh, go grr yourself." Nina laughed and rolled to sit on the edge of the bed. "Alright you… I'm going to go to the grocery store and you're going to stay here. We can't live off of bad burgers and beef jerky forever and I'm pretty sure the store doesn't want you in there eating everything you can get your paws on."

Nina stood and scooped up Aki's water bowl. She refilled it and placed it on the floor by the bed. Aki hopped down to examine it and lost interest upon realizing it was only water. Nina grabbed her sweatshirt and threw on her shoes while Aki watched with keen interest. As she moved to the door he followed close behind.

"No, Aki, you need to stay."

Aki began to whimper and wind himself around her legs. Nina took care to step over him and keep her body between Aki and the outdoors.

"I'll be right back. I promise."

Nina managed to squeeze out the door without letting Aki out with her. As she walked down the hall, the curtain of their room jostled. She looked back to see the tips of Aki's paws and his nose poking through, pushed up against the glass. The sight of it warmed her and hit her with a pang of sadness at the same time. They had bonded quite a bit over the last few days.

Nina took her time wandering the aisles of the grocery store. She felt calm. Calmer than she had in years. She took a moment to inhale the scent of roasting chicken at the deli and to admire the fresh strawberries bursting out of their cartons. She slowed her cart to let a bedraggled mother and her overflowing cart complete with two young children step into line in front of her at the checkout. It was all so normal. She had forgotten what normal was like. How good it felt.

As she loaded her groceries into the back seat of the truck, she felt the corner of the paper bag snag the seat cushion. With a good shove, the bag slid over into the middle seat, but Nina realized that the seat cushion in front of her had been knocked loose in the process. She struggled to push it back into place, but the cushion refused to budge.

"Well, that's definitely not supposed to happen," Nina grumbled to herself. "This truck must be old as..."

The words caught in Nina's throat as she noticed the carpet peeling back at the base of the seat. Suspiciously new carpeting. Nina raised a hesitant hand and slid her fingers into the gap in the upholstery. A few sharp tugs got it loose, revealing massive bundles of cash and several bricks of cocaine. For a surreal moment, Nina's hand drifted to one of the bricks. Her fingernails traced the thin plastic. She remembered how it felt, the freeing rush that accompanied her benders, how she felt like she was flying until the day the elders had asked her to move off the reservation. To leave her family and life behind. She had brought them nothing but sickness, addiction, and fear courtesy of her then-new boyfriend, Savin. She chose cocaine over her family, her home... and cocaine never made her fly again. But maybe now... now that she had been clean for so long...

"No," Nina said a little too loudly. The mother who had passed her earlier looked up from the car seat she was attempting to buckle in her SUV. Nina gave her an awkward wave and slammed the back door shut. She scurried back to the driver's seat and peeled the truck out of the parking lot before the poor mother had time to process what she'd seen.

***

Out in the ocean, the sky darkened as thunder clouds and winds developed, sending a large choppy wave rolling in behind Charlie. Just in time, he slipped back out of the wave as it broke into white water early. He positioned himself once again to catch his last wave in and call it a day.

Waves generally come in sets or groups of waves. In between that time, the ocean is often quiet. Today was barely an exception, other than it being slightly bumpier than usual from the storm approaching. Charlie found the gentle rocking of the sea somewhat soothing as he waited. His mind wandered as he drifted.

He couldn't stop thinking about that beautiful woman and her slightly scruffy dog. Katera and Aki. He wondered if he would ever see them again. The attraction he felt for her was unlike anything he had felt in a really long time, perhaps ever. He couldn't figure out what it was about her that intrigued him so much. Maybe, it was just the way she looked at him. In her eyes, there was something about her that was equally strong, vulnerable and undeniably complicated.

Charlie didn't shy away from complications or challenges. Life always seemed to send him challenges. After his injury to his knee, life suddenly seemed to have no meaning. Surfing was everything to Charlie. He wasn't a champion surfer anymore. Without that, he wondered if he had any purpose at all. Would he really mean anything to anyone? If it were not for his mentor and friend, the surfing legend, Nalu, he was certain he may not be alive today. He believed in Charlie. He helped him reconnect with the sea, and taught him the art of surfboard shaping. This gave him purpose again. In the end, Nalu was more than just someone he looked up to, he was like a father to him, much more than his real father ever was.

"The sea is like… life," Nalu would say. "Each wave is pushed by the wind and currents, from miles away. It all connects, like time. What happened in the past connects to what is now… So, the question is… do you surf *that* wave? Or do you let it pass? Sometimes, as with life… there is no choice. The wave is coming whether you are ready or not. You *must* ride the wave, because it is within us. We must try to understand it… And then, you will know who you really are and where you need to be."

Charlie took a deep breath in as Nalu's words echoed in his memory.

The smell of the sea engulfed him. This was still *his* place. His beach. His ocean. He rubbed his knee in response to his thoughts, and then he spun his board around to watch the incoming surf.

The thought of that beautiful woman and her dog snuck back into his mind again for a moment but it quickly vanished as the distant sound of thunder cracked. He knew what that meant. Time to get the next wave in.

Right on cue, there was a huge set of choppy waves coming right towards him. He readied his board. He knew those waves would not be easy to roll out of. He would need to surf them in.

Nina raced through the motel room gathering her things and shoving them back in the duffel bag. Aki watched her without comment. He could sense her stress. Aki hopped into the passenger seat while Nina loaded up the car and cocked his head at her when she plopped down in the driver's seat to double-check she had not forgotten anything. Aki gave a small bark as if to remind Nina of her own urgency.

"Ah yes. I got you something, Aki."

Aki's ears perked up as Nina rummaged through one of the grocery bags. She pulled out a brand-new blue collar and leash. Aki held still and allowed Nina to clasp the collar around his neck.

"Well don't you look handsome?" Nina gave Aki a weary smile. "Now everyone who sees you will know you are someone. You belong with someone." Nina gave Aki a gentle hug.

Aki responded with a low "hruff," which Nina took as his stamp of approval. And with that, they were back on the road.

Rain began to come down. Nina turned on the truck's old windshield wipers. Aki found them slightly annoying as they screeched and scratched as they wiped.

Suddenly, thunder cracked. Aki shuttered from the sound.

"It's ok. Aki. It's just thunder. Nothing to be afraid of."

Aki wasn't totally convinced, curling up in a tight ball and shivering. He shook so violently that Nina wondered if he was just scared or if he was having a medical emergency, like a stroke or a seizure.

As they continued on their way out of town, Nina drove right by the road to the beach. Aki's head whipped around to stare after it. He shuffled in his seat and looked from Nina to the receding drive. Nina tried to ignore his gaze, but Aki refused to look away. When Nina turned to face him, she was once again startled by the blaze of empathy and intellect in his eyes. It *wasn't* difficult to discern what he wanted Nina to do. The rain nor thunder didn't seem to concern Aki much anymore. His eyes were focused on the road toward Charlie's place.

Nina slammed on the breaks and let the car idle in the road for a moment. Aki waited patiently, simply *staring* at her. Nina threw her head back against the seat and closed her eyes.

"Well FINE then. If you're going to be so damn loud about it."

And they were on their way back to Charlie's.

★★★

The rain had eased up a bit as they pulled into the beach parking lot in front of Charlie's beach house and surf shop. Aki leapt from the truck the moment Nina opened the passenger door and made a beeline for Charlie's house. Nina smiled in spite of herself and her situation. She was just going to say goodbye. She was going to thank him for the meal, apologize for her awkwardness, and then say goodbye to Charlie for once and for all. She rehearsed her words in her head as Aki ran for the door. Then he stopped short. His nose went up and he turned in a small circle. He cocked his head towards the beach and began to jog off in that direction.

"Hey Aki, come on! We don't have time for a swim. Or for seagull chasing."

Aki stopped and hesitantly turned back and trotted to Nina. Nina knocked on Charlie's door, but no reply came.

"Charlie? Are you home? It's Ni—It's Katera. Charlie?"

Again, there was no answer.

"Oh… well… I would have liked to say goodbye, but we should keep moving," Nina said to Aki, struggling to disguise the lump in her throat. "Come on, boy."

Nina headed back toward the truck, but Aki moved toward the beach, trotting with purpose.

"Aki, come on! We don't have time for this…"

With that, Aki took off running toward the beach.

"Aki, no! Stop!"

Nina gave chase. She was surprised to find that she was able to keep up with Aki this time. It was as though he ran slowly enough that he knew she'd be able to keep pace but too fast for her to catch him.

It's like he wants me to follow him... Nina thought in between huffs of air.

Nina came tumbling through the dunes after Aki, only just keeping her footing. Aki was flying toward the water. Toward a lump of driftwood by the water. Toward a lump of driftwood that kind of looked like—

"Charlie!!" Nina screamed.

She was by his side in seconds. Aki paced anxiously next to them.

"What happened? Where are you hurt?"

Charlie groaned and propped himself up on his elbows.

"It's my damn knee. A monster wave knocked me off my board and wrenched it. I was the last one out there. I thought I was going to be on this beach all night..."

Charlie brushed his hair from his eyes and tried to smile at her. A red stream of blood followed his fingers.

"You've hit your head too. You're bleeding!"

Charlie struggled to stand. "I'll be fine. Just a scratch."

"Hold on, let me help you."

Nina ducked under Charlie's arm and helped him to his feet. The two began a slow shuffle up the sand toward his house.

"What the hell were you doing out here so late?"

Charlie attempted to flash his light-hearted smile. "Waiting for you."

CHAPTER 11

— SECOND CHANCES —

Nina grabbed gauze, tape, and rubbing alcohol from Charlie's medicine cabinet. Despite his claims that the cut was 'nothing,' Charlie let out a muffled yelp and dug his fingers into the couch when Nina dabbed some of the rubbing alcohol on it. Once the wound was clean and covered, Nina moved to wrap Charlie's leg. He stopped her and held his hand out for the athletic tape.

"I think you need a doctor." Nina said as she reluctantly handed over the tape.

"Don't worry, I've done this dozens of times before. I'll be good in a day or two. I'm a pro. Besides, I need to shower first. Help me to the bathroom?"

Nina helped him ease himself off the couch into a standing position. Aki flitted about them, unsure how to help. With her free hand, Nina gave Aki a soothing pat.

"So… did you come back to see me?"

"I… came back to say goodbye actually. We're on our way up north."

"Oh… I see."

Nina and Charlie avoided eye contact as Nina transferred her share of Charlie's weight to the bathroom counter. When she shut the door behind her, Nina could here Charlie hopping across the room.

"You alright in there?"

"I'm fine, thank you."

Charlie's words were followed by the distinct sound of a shower caddy hitting the tile floor.

"... Still fine."

Nina shouted back, "Ok, well since you're *fine* in there, I'm going to start making dinner out here."

Nina quietly mumbled to herself in a self-imposed scolding while she tried to figure out what to prepare for dinner. "What the hell am I thinking?!"

Nina shook her head at this entire situation, as she mocked herself. "I'm going to make dinner... Oh my god... Dinner?!!"

Aki joined in with a playful bark, because he obviously thought it was a GREAT idea.

"What? Oh... I know YOU like this."

Nina peaked around Charlie's kitchen for all the right things to cook a meal. His cupboard and fridge didn't bear much to offer. There were very few meals she actually knew how to cook. She remembered cooking many traditional Navajo meals with her mother when she was younger. But she didn't have the ingredients for that. Not really. But she knew she had chicken and few other basic fixings in her truck. She even bought some kale. "That sounds kind of surfer-healthy." She thought.

She stepped out to the truck that she had *borrowed*, and grabbed the large bag of groceries that she had just purchased with *the drug money she stole from her ex-boyfriend*.... She did her best to shake that thought out of her head, at least for tonight.

Nina marched back into the kitchen with the grocery bag in hand, whispering to Aki as if he should understand everything she had to say, "Do you know how dangerous this all is?" Or perhaps she was just talking to herself.

Aki just huffed. Nina responded back. "We NEED to get a..."

Before she could get that full sentence out, Charlie appeared all cleaned up and more handsome than ever. If that was even possible, she pondered. His muscled and tan chest peaked through his Hawaiian shirt as he buttoned it up. He left the top two buttons undone. Surfer casual style.

"What do you need?" he asked.

"Oh, wow. That was fast." Nina stammered as she caught the full image of Charlie in all of his ridiculously handsome glory.

Charlie smiled. "Do you need something? I know I don't have that much in the fridge ...."

Nina was almost speechless again.

"No. I'm good. I have what I need to make dinner. Just sit down and rest. Ok?"

Charlie smiled as he limped over to the couch. "You don't have to do this if you don't want to. It's ok."

"It's the least I can do after you served us your 'famous Huevo Rancheros'. I may not cook you something as great as that, so don't thank me quite yet."

Dinner was a rather quiet affair, at first. Nina and Charlie were awkward: reaching for the same utensils, starting to talk at the same time, staring and looking away when the other noticed. Aki gave a disgruntled bark to let her know that he had not received his portion of the meal. Nina was grateful for the excuse to leave the table and hurried to share some of her food with Aki. She plopped some chicken along with kale salad into Aki's bowl.

"You know…," Charlie began, "I don't recall having any kale in my fridge."

"I had some groceries in my car."

"I thought you weren't staying."

"Plans change."

Charlie smiled. "Something good out of something bad," he murmured.

Before Nina could respond, a harsh hacking sound could be heard from next to the table. Aki looked up from the kale salad at Nina with disgust evident on his face. Both Nina and Charlie began to laugh, the last of the tension floating away.

"Hey, we can't have 'world famous' huevo rancheros for every meal," Nina teased.

***

Early the next morning, Nina was jostled from her peaceful slumber on the couch by the shadow of a man. Before panic could overtake her, Charlie's face pushed forward through the fog induced gloom. In the early morning light, his features had adopted a softer edge, bringing his good looks to another level. He looked otherworldly to Nina.

Nina brushed the remainder of the sleep from her eyes. "Hey, you shouldn't be walking around on that knee. Can I get something for you?"

From his crouched position by the couch, Charlie leaned in closer and did not answer. He brushed a strand of hair from Nina's cheek.

"I... You don't know me..." Nina tried, weakly. She had trouble forming words when he was looking at her like that.

Charlie slid his hand under her chin and gently tipped her face up to meet his. He couldn't look away. She was the most beautiful woman he had ever seen.

Nina couldn't recall leaning forward to meet Charlie. It was instinctual. As soon as their lips met the rest of the world disappeared. She grabbed hold of the waist of his shorts and tugged him onto the couch with her. He pulled back to look at her, as if to be certain of her longing.

He removed his shirt. His eyes met hers. She gently traced her finger tips over his tan muscled abdomen. His breath quivered. He returned her touch with his strong embrace. He wrapped his arms around her and pulled her close, his mouth hungry for her, but he stopped right before reaching her. His lips were so close to hers, but he would not kiss her. He held on to her. Their breath in sync. She trembled with desire.

Like the whisper of the wind on the ocean, Charlie slid his thumb underneath her bra. This was the moment. The feeling that she had longed for. The feeling of acceptance. As his thumb slid down to her rib cage, she could not breathe. She could not move. She inhaled his scent. It was just her and Charlie. Her heart was beating so fast. She knew Charlie could feel it. He had a gentle, magical touch. Was this real? She peered up. His eyes were warm with desire. She leaned up.

She wanted to be loved. She wanted to be rescued. She was ready to give herself to him.

Finally, as if he felt her complete desire, his skin against her skin, hers against his…. Intertwined, unable to tell whose limbs were whose. The room was filled with a pale blue glow that made Nina feel as though they would live in that place for eternity. They were the only people who mattered. As her eyes closed, he pulled her even tighter, pressing his body into hers.

And at that moment, a man named James Savin had never existed.

***

"Stay with me. And not just for another night."

Nina set her coffee back down on the table as she struggled not to choke on it. Charlie stared across the table at her. His earnest face made her throat tighten. How could she possibly explain to this man, this lovely, lovely man, that she not only had to leave for both of their sakes, but that she was nowhere near the woman he thought she was?

"Charlie, I really need to—"

"Stay with me? I agree." Charlie quipped with a smirk. Nina frowned.

"You don't know me."

"We might have to agree to disagree there. Where are you in such a rush to get off to anyways?"

"I don't know. I really don't know."

The smile slid right off Charlie's face. His brow furrowed with concern. He leaned forward and clasped Nina's hand in his own. Nina fought not to melt at his touch.

"What are you running from?"

"I just—nothing... I don't know."

Charlie's brow relaxed just a bit. He didn't quite believe her, but he wasn't going to push it. Scraping his chair back, Charlie limped around the table to Nina and leaned against the table.

"Then stay. I've never met anyone like you, and I don't want to let you go."

He leaned in before Nina could object again. And when he kissed her, Nina found she no longer had the strength or the desire to put her objections to words.

In his bed, he made love to her again, with a passion that neither of them had ever felt before. It was complete. She felt safe. Nina allowed herself to feel his love. She relinquished all of her hesitations, all of her fears. She allowed herself to fill a need, a thirst for love and a connection that she had no idea could exist until now. She feared that this one moment in time may never last. That it might be the only time in her life that she will truly feel this way. So, she made love to him back, with all that was real, all that was her... with passion and urgency.

CHAPTER 12

— TRUTH AND PENANCE —

A black hummer with gold plated hubcaps tore across the Motel-6 parking lot, screeching to a halt across three separate parking spaces. The hummer's horn let out a frustrated blare as Quintero punched the wheel.

"The app says the truck should be here. It's says it's right fucking there!" Quintero pointed to an empty spot across from the hummer where the truck, very clearly, was not.

"Could be that the battery in the tracker died." Savin interjected, trying to at least sound helpful.

"Could be. Or it could be that your girlfriend planned this. A wild goose chase to distract us while she takes off with my drugs and money. Could it be that, Savin?"

Savin didn't have to turn his head to know that Quintero had once again placed his gun against Savin's temple. He tried to ignore the cool circular barrel pressed against his skin and gritted his teeth. He could not show fear. Not in front of Quintero. It would be as good as signing his death certificate.

"We WILL find her. She can't be that far away."

"She could be anywhere now, estupido!"

Savin felt sweat begin to roll down his hairline. As he scrambled to come up with something that would reassure Quintero, Savin caught sight of a stout maid pushing a cart stepping out of a room on the second floor of the motel.

"Look!"

Savin bounded out of the hummer and up the motel stairs towards the maid with Quintero right on his heels.

"Hey, lady," Savin shouted.

The maid spun around and gasped at the sight of the two large men moving toward her. Her fear froze her in place.

"Have you seen her?"

Savin held up his phone to show the maid a picture of Nina. The maid nodded slowly and pointed to the room Nina had occupied the day before.

"She gone?"

The maid nodded.

"She coming back?"

The maid shook her head. Quintero uttered an animal-like growl behind Savin. The maid took a half step back, ready to run. Savin felt his heart drop.

"Fuck! Uhm… wait. Have you cleaned it yet?"

The maid shook her head.

"Good. Open it."

***

"It was right here! I swear to god it was right here!"

Cortez watched Davis pace the beach parking space that, according to the drone footage, should have been holding the truck they had been tracking. After questioning some of the locals, Cortez and Davis had come across a couple who claimed to have seen a woman matching Nina's description chasing a dog down a local beach. Davis had been doing sweeps of the beach since then, on the off-chance Nina returned with the truck. Not twenty minutes ago, Cortez had seen it there, with her own eyes, on Davis' monitor. And now it was gone.

"She must have left in the time it took us to drive here." Cortez sighed. "Give it up, Davis. We can go back to our hotel and keep an eye on this spot with the drone."

A bewildered Davis clambered back into Cortez's black Camaro. As she punched the gas, Davis was thrown back in his seat.

"Remind me why we took your car and not the surveillance van? I could be back in the sky right now, getting a jump on our girl. But nooooo we gotta wait until you stop the car so I can get my equipment set up"

"Speed, Davis. Speed."

***

Nina couldn't stop thinking about the last 48 hours. What had happened? Charlie was someone that she never expected. Was it real or some sort of imagined dream? A surfer? What in the world? Okay… He's incredibly handsome, but still…

Nina drove her truck through the streets of Ventura County Beach with determination as she contemplated her situation.

She had told Charlie that she would be back in a couple of hours. She *would* come back to him. She was only running a few errands. She left Aki *with* Charlie. And of course, Aki thought that was perfectly fine.

Why did Aki trust Charlie so? Nina pondered. Such a curious dog, she realized. Then she had to admit, she had the same affliction. She too, was compelled to say that Charlie seemed pretty darn perfect.

Nina found an open parking spot right in front, and maneuvered the old truck to prepare to move into it. This was only going to take a few minutes, she thought. This would be the answer to everything. She parked the truck and entered the post office.

***

Cortez flew down the coastal highway back in the direction of main street and their hotel. Davis didn't say it, but the way Cortez wove through traffic made him nauseous.

"I'm just saying. For future field trips, I would like to formally request that we use the surveillance van. Sure, your

Camaro is faster, but I could have found Nina Locklear by now if..."

"If you opened your eyes and had a little faith." Cortez interjected. "Look!"

A couple hundred yards ahead of them, the truck was parked outside a post office. As Cortez swerved into a parking spot, Nina appeared in the post office doorway.

Cortez was out of the car before it had fully rolled to a halt.

"Nina!"

Nina did not turn towards her name. Instead, she turned and sped-walked in the opposite direction.

"Nina Locklear, FBI!" Cortez shouted forcefully as Davis jogged to catch up with her.

Nina stopped in her tracks. Her heart sank. Every breath she ever took, had left her body. She made a slow about-face and Cortez made eye contact. Nina's face could be read as nothing short of terrified. Cortez and Davis pulled out their badges to show Nina and then tucked them away. No need to alert any civilians.

"Nina, I'm Agent Cortez and this is Agent Davis. We're here to help you."

"You can't help me. There is nothing anyone can do to help me."

Davis rushed to correct her. "We know everything! We know about Savin's drug and arm deals as well as the dog fights. All we need is someone like you to testify and bring him down! We can protect you, Nina. If you help us, we can protect you."

"Aren't you listening? You CAN NOT protect me! Not from him. And if you're not going to arrest me then I'm going to need you to leave me alone."

Nina pushed past Cortez and made a beeline for her truck. Cortez wracked her brain, desperate to latch onto something that would make Nina stay.

"You took a dog."

Nina stopped fumbling with her keys but remained silent.

"You were home free. We saw you from our drone. You made it to the truck, started the engine, but then you got out and ran to the warehouse to get that dog. You risked your life for him. Why?"

Nina's lip trembled, and she clutched the keys tight in her fist. "Because he matters," she whispered. Then she turned on her heel to face the agents.

"I matter. Savin treated me like I was nothing, like I was his property. But we are not items to be possessed! That dog could no longer fight. He was going to die as a bait dog the next night. Do you have any idea how horrific of a death he was in for? So, yes, I took him. He's still with me too. He is my friend. His name's Aki. And I'd do it all again."

It was clear Nina was working hard to keep her voice from breaking. Cortez reached out a comforting hand, but Nina jerked away.

Davis stepped forward with his palms raised. "Nina, we have intelligence that suggests Savin is on his way here to find you. You're not safe."

"That's what I've been trying to tell you." Nina said with a bitter laugh, but both agents saw the panic register in her eyes. "So, if you're not going to arrest me, please, just get out of my way."

Nina moved to open the door to the truck and Cortez stepped in to block her. Nina opened her mouth to start shouting, but Cortez quickly extended a card.

"In case you should change your mind, that's all." Cortez said as she stepped back.

Nina gave her a gruff nod and swung the driver's door open. She turned the engine and was halfway down the street in the blink of an eye.

"Well, crap. Now what?" Davis moaned, defeated.

"Now, we get the drone."

Davis didn't need to be told twice. He ran to the Camaro and had his drone tailing the truck before Cortez had time to crack a joke about speed mattering more than size.

CHAPTER 13

—— TRUTH AND VENGEANCE ——

She pushed down harder on the accelerator of the old truck as she played back what had just happened in her mind. It had been such a perfect night and an even better morning. She should have known it was too good to last. Tears began to fill her eyes as her anger and fear mingled as she reminisced.

She had walked into the post office on a cloud, replaying her morning with Charlie over and over. Once they had finished breakfast, and made love once again. Nina had gone out and retrieved the pieces of the broken surfboard Charlie had been forced to leave behind on the beach. She brought them to his workshop, and there, she had insisted he try to fix it, despite his insistence that it was a lost cause.

At Nina's request, they soon found themselves back in the workshop and Charlie agreed to take a crack at mending the board. Charlie talked Nina through every move he made and involved her in every way he could, guiding her hands over the board, carefully patching the ding, and helping her shift the power tools along to sand it down smoothly. He let her attach new fins on her own, indicating where they needed to be fastened and how to go about it. In just a few hours, the board was practically new again, it's fiberglass gleaming as it showed off its new design, a single gorgeous eagle feather.

"It's incredible," Nina smiled and pressed her cheek to Charlie's shoulder. "You're a magnificent artist."

Charlie slid her into his arms and kissed her cheek. "It's better than it was before. Because of you."

Nina pushed into his embrace and kissed him hard. He wrapped her tightly in his arms by way of reply. Nina almost felt like she was flying…and her breath hitched in her throat. It was like when she was on drugs, when she was drunk.

Her whole body tingled and buzzed with joy, her thoughts not totally clear. She was flying, high and without worry or fear. She wanted to stay like this forever and her whole body ached for more.

Only this time she was drunk on a feeling, swept away by what she could only surmise was love. Not the love that Savin claimed he had, the fake love he pretended to bestow on her. No, that was just fake - cheap, like the homemade wine some people at the reservation once tried to make. This feeling…this was the *real* stuff.

Nina realized with a start that this feeling, being intoxicated by joy and hope and love, was better than she had ever felt before. It was better than the rush she got from cocaine, better than the drawn-out dreamland that tequila kept her in.

Because for once, this dreamland was bordering on being real.

But her dreams of a life with a man like Charlie came screeching to a halt at that post office just moments ago. Her world was shattered when she heard the cry of Agent Cortez. The agent's voice cracked like a whip through her happy memory, bringing her crashing back to Earth with her own name: "Nina!"

She had tried to flee, but it was no use. They were on her in seconds. They knew her name. They knew about Savin. They even knew she had Aki. And they had found her. Across two state lines, they had found her. And if they could find her... Agent Davis' words echoed in her ears: "intelligence suggests Savin is on his way here to find you..."

The truck's engine roared below her. No one had asked it to drive more than sixty miles an hour in years. It wasn't even capable of the eighty that Nina was demanding of it. Even as she floored it, the speedometer refused to budge past seventy-two. Nina cursed the old engine. She wiped tears from her face and struggled to keep her breathing steady. She needed to get back to Charlie and come clean. She needed to beg for his forgiveness, his understanding. And then she and Aki needed to run.

Nina took little notice of the black hummer on the other side of the parking lot as she drove to the edge near Charlie's house. It wasn't until she realized the front door was ajar that she understood she was too late. Her hand hovered over the doorknob, unable to proceed. Then Nina heard Aki's panicked bark from inside and she forced herself to enter.

"Charlie? Charlie!!"

There he was at the kitchen table, bound, gagged, and bloody. Aki was nowhere to be seen, but Nina could hear his frantic scratching at the bedroom door. Nina ran to get to Charlie but was stopped when someone grabbed hold of a fistful of her hair and threw her to the ground. Nina smacked her head hard. As the world flickered in front of her, Nina heard her ex-boyfriend's vile voice, dripping with condescension.

"You really need to get better at cleaning up after yourself, babe."

Savin's face appeared through the dark spots that clouded her vision.

Savin's face drifted out of view. And then Nina's whole body was on fire. Nina would have screamed, but she found she could not draw air. The sound of electricity crackling was deafening, punctuated only by Aki's continued barking. Nina thrashed on the floor, and then briefly released from pain just in time to see Savin pull the cattle prod away… so he could swing it at her face.

Nina's vision went dark again. Aki's distant barks melded with Charlie's muffled shouts. Savin's malicious laugh rose above the din and Nina felt the cattle prod strike her across the chest. With what little vision she had regained, Nina crawled away from Savin. He followed after her, shocking her every few steps, until she found herself pushed up against the wall. Savin crouched to face her.

Nina faintly pleaded. "Stop..."

"You stole my dog. You stole a fuck-ton of money and drugs. And you had the fucking audacity to think you could walk away from me. So, what shall I do to you? What punishment is worthy of those crimes?" Savin bellowed as he lashed out with the cattle prod again. "Why. Should. I. STOP?"

Each word was accompanied by a shock from the prod. Aki let out a whine of recognition at the noise. Nina was able to collect her thoughts enough to feel terrible for exposing Aki to this man again. And not only Aki but Charlie... Where was Charlie?

Nina inched out of her fetal position, managing to sit herself up against the wall in between jabs. There he was! Through her fuzzy vision, Nina could still make out Charlie's muscular form, straining against his binds at the kitchen table. Savin followed her gaze.

"Ohhhh is this your new 'boyfriend' Nina? Tell me, does he know all about you? Have you filled him in on everything that makes you, 'you,' my little squaw?"

Nina tried desperately to apologize with her eyes. Charlie could only answer back with wide-eyed confusion.

"I... I-I'm s-sorry, Charlie." Nina managed to whisper. Charlie looked away, brow furrowed.

"Did she tell you I gave her everything she ever wanted? Hmm? Did she lover boy? She LOVED being with me. Girl can drink with the best of 'em. Suck up bumps the size of ski slopes. I gave it all to her and SHE LOVES IT!"

Nina closed her eyes, no longer able to stand meeting Charlie's.

A bang sounded out from the bedroom. Then another. Aki was throwing himself against the door at the sound of the "bad-man's" voice. Aki knew that voice and the sound of the cattle prod all too well.

"Money, drugs, alcohol, I gave it all… But she didn't like me hurting the doggies. That's where she drew the line, of all places. You know what? Maybe it makes sense, considering she's an ungrateful BITCH!"

Savin strode across the room and banged twice on the bedroom door. Aki stopped barking, surprised by the sound.

"You know I could have killed him when I got here. I really would have loved to see your face… But! He still needs to fight for me. He owes me. I'm not done with him yet. You on the other hand…"

Savin stalked back across the room to Nina. He wrapped both hands around her throat and lifted her up against the wall. Nina began to choke, and the sound caused Aki to begin barking even louder than before. Nina forced herself to look into Savin's eyes, desperate to find whatever small scrap of humanity had stopped him from killing her before. But all she saw was darkness.

Charlie strained heavily on the binding around his wrists. He twisted and cranked his arms to the point that they could almost dislocate. He felt the ties loosen slightly, enough to slide one hand free. He glared at Savin as he choked on the gag tightly stuffed in his mouth.

"Res... Rat..." Savin hissed at Nina, his whole body shaking with the effort of holding her off the ground by her throat.

"I told you I would kill—"

A crack rang out as one of Charlie's surfing trophies made contact with the back of Savin's head. Savin and Nina tumbled to the ground, Savin unconscious and Nina gasping for air. A bare foot rolled Savin's body out of the way. Nina looked up to see Charlie towering over them, trophy in hand. His face revealed his emotions with equal parts concern, confusion, anger and pain. He ripped the gag out of his mouth and released some blood tinged spit.

"What is going on?" he blurted out, as he examined the laceration Savin's cattle prod had left across her face. "You stole drugs? You lied to me?"

"No... I didn't.... I didn't mean to lie... It's not that simple," Nina whispered, her voice hoarse. "I tried to tell you... I was coming here to tell you..."

"Who are you? Katera? Nina?"

"I'm *Nina*."

"We need to call the police." Charlie moved toward the landline on his kitchen counter.

"I wouldn't do that if I were you." Savin's voice sounded like a snake preparing to strike.

Nina and Charlie both turned to see Savin rising from the floor, one hand on the back of his head, the other pointing a handgun at Charlie. Savin seemed shaky, but remarkably unphased by his abrupt meeting with the floor. Savin smirked at Nina.

"What, you thought I'd show up without a gun?"

Charlie launched himself across the room at Savin without hesitation, knocking the gun from his hand and sending it skittering across the floor. The two tumbled to the floor swinging, both men out for blood. Savin took the upper hand and leapt on top of Charlie, but a sharp left hook from Charlie had him on the ground in seconds. Savin made a desperate scramble in the direction the gun had gone, but Charlie grabbed him by the back of the collar and slid him back. He wrapped Savin in a choke hold, pressing his forearm into his neck.

"Asshole!" Charlie shouted into Savin's ear.

Incensed, Savin twisted his neck far enough to line up his mouth with Charlie's forearm and chomped down.

"AGHHH."

As Charlie loosened his grip, Savin kicked out from under him and got to his feet. Charlie tried to follow suit, but Savin, having clocked Charlie's limp, took him down with a swift kick to the knee. Charlie crashed to the ground with a moan. Savin gave him a swift kick to the liver for good measure, leaving Charlie gagging.

"Amateur…" Savin scoffed. "This is just too much fun!"

Savin spun around to collect his gun, only to find Nina had beaten him to it. Nina's hands shook as she aimed the gun. Just a side effect of the cattle prod, Nina told herself. The flash of fear that crossed Savin's face was replaced with smug satisfaction. He strolled forward and held his hand out to Nina.

"Come on, little squaw. We both know you don't have the balls to sh—"

Bang!

Savin leapt back from the warning shot Nina landed at his feet.

"You little bi—"

"What the hell is going on in here?"

Nina looked up in surprise to see another man glowering in the doorway. It took a moment for Nina to recognize Quintero, but when she did, she felt the color flood from her face. Savin whirled around to face his boss.

"I'm trying to kill my ex-girlfriend, do you mind?" Savin snapped.

"Not yet." Quintero snarled.

"The fuck do you mean, 'not yet?' You have the truck, right? So, I get the girl!"

Quintero crossed to Savin and grabbed him by the shirt collar. "I said you'd get the girl when I got back my truck with everything in it. EVERYTHING ISN'T IN IT."

Nina watched Savin's face pale. His anger at her had momentarily made him forget his fear of Quintero. Savin gave Quintero a silent nod and he let go of Savin's shirt.

"Babe," Savin began with a frigid smile, "where did you put the money and drugs?"

Nina looked from Savin to Quintero.

"I'll tell you. But only if you let Charlie go."

Charlie made an attempt to stand at Nina's words, but his knee, now dark purple and the size of a grapefruit, kept him on the ground.

"Nina—" Charlie whispered.

'Aww well isn't that sweet. You know I can't do that." Savin spit out.

"Let him GO!" Nina bellowed. She stepped forward and pointed the gun straight at Savin's head. Savin's eyes seethed with rage, but before he could speak, the silence was filled by Quintero's laughter.

"Savin, is that *your* gun?"

Startled by the question, Savin looked from Quintero to the gun in Nina's hand.

"Oh, well, yeah. I guess so."

Quintero laughed harder. "Oh boy, this little girl turned your own gun on you! Hahaha…"

Quintero wiped a tear of laughter from his eye and turned to Nina, still chuckling. "Senorita, you know my gun is bigger than his gun, right?"

Quintero swung the strap of his uzi around so that the gun was trained on Nina. He unloaded a couple rapid rounds into the floor by her feet to make his point. Nina lowered Savin's gun to the ground and slid it across the floor.

"Much better. Now tell me where you put my property, or I'll blow a crater in your pretty little—"

He was cut off. A voice echoed through the room, a familiar voice. Nina felt her blood run cold, out of fear of more people who would now die because of her. She willed it to go away, squeezed her eyes shut, and tried not to hear the crackled voice that rang out from a bullhorn.

"Eduardo Quintero, this is Agent Cortez with the FBI. We know you are in there and we have the building surrounded. Come out with your hands up!"

***

Cortez and Davis stood behind their respective car doors, guns trained on the entrance to Charlie's house, which they had seen Quintero disappear through as they pulled up to the parking lot. Cortez could hear Davis' gun tapping against the car. She wished he would steady his hand.

"Are you sure this is a good idea?"

"You saw him walking in there. You heard the gunshots. We had to intervene."

"Yes, but what if he calls our—"

A spray of gunfire erupted through Charlie's front door and both agents ducked down for cover.

"And this is why I wanted to wait for back-up!" Davis shrieked over the din of the ricocheting bullets.

***

Quintero fired with reckless abandon through Charlie's front door in the general direction of Cortez's voice. Nina had warned them. She could not be saved, and now they couldn't either. Savin stepped up next to Quintero and began firing through the almost-obliterated door. Sharp cracks rang out from outside and Quintero and Savin hit the floor. Nina followed their lead and crawled over to Charlie.

The two ducked their heads and curled up together as debris rained down around them. Chunks of wood, plaster, and glass clattered to the floor. The machine gun roared. Nina could hear Aki's barks rise in pitch. He resumed thrusting his body against the bedroom door.

***

Cortez gestured for Davis to change positions and follow her over to the heavy wood door of Charlie's workshop. She shoved Davis behind the door just as another bullet whizzed over her shoulder.

"You must take me for a fool," Quintero spat in disgust. Cortez peeked around the door to see Quintero holding Charlie up with the uzi trained on his head. Next to him, Savin clutched Nina with his handgun against her temple. Through a window just behind the four, Cortez noticed a furry streak whipping back and forth. When he realized, his human companions had moved outside, Aki began to bark ferociously at the window and clawed at the glass. It appeared the dog cared as much for Nina as she did for him. Cortez cleared her throat, shaking the sweet thought, and shouted over to Quintero.

"Let them go, Quintero. This isn't the way to handle things."

Quintero glanced from Cortez's hiding spot to his hummer. "We're leaving now. You better not follow."

"You don't want to do that. No need to add kidnapping to your charges."

"HA. Kidnapping? That is nothing."

Cortez watched Savin's face drop at her words. Quintero was too ruthless to care. But she might be able to get Savin to try and save his own hide.

"We gotta move, Quintero." Savin urged his boss. He gave Nina a shove forward as he spoke. Nina stumbled and fell to the ground under the force of Savin's shove. Savin leaned down and, grabbing Nina by her hair, yanked her to her feet. Nina screamed as she felt the hair ripped from her scalp and gun digging into her cheek.

"Stop!!" Charlie shouted.

"Shut up!" Savin snapped back at him. Nina's legs shook beneath her. "Stand UP you lazy sack of shit!" Savin roared.

With that, Aki had enough. The "bad-man" was hurting his Nina. In one flying leap, Aki came crashing through the window, teeth bared, eyes locked on Savin. Aki closed the distance between them in seconds and sank his teeth deep into Savin's forearm, thrashing wildly.

"AGHHHHH!!" Savin wailed in pain. Firing at random, Savin was unable to line up a shot at Aki while Aki ripped apart his gun wielding arm. Seeing this, Quintero shoved Charlie to the ground and grabbed Nina as his new hostage. Nina twisted in Quintero's arms, desperate to keep her eyes on Aki. She managed to crane her neck around just in time to see Savin toss the gun into his free hand and turn it on Aki.

Bang!

"NO!!!" Nina screamed. "Aki!"

Aki dropped to the ground, motionless. Savin writhed in pain from his mangled arm. Tears streamed from Nina's eyes.

Clocking Savin's inability to fight and hearing the distant sound of sirens approaching, Quintero abandoned Savin and opened fire on the agents as he backed toward his car, dragging Nina. With a scream of agony, Charlie launched himself to his feet and grabbed Quintero around the waist, tearing him away from Nina. Quintero shook himself free of the injured man with ease, knocking Charlie to the ground, and whipping the uzi around to take aim. Nina saw the world slow to almost a stand still as she registered what was about to happen. Quintero's finger squeezed down on the trigger of his uzi. Right before her eyes, Charlie was about to die. The man she had fallen in love with. It was all about to end in a millisecond, and it was all her fault. Before Charlie could stop her, Nina launched herself in front of Quintero's gun. Bullets ripped through her torso and sent fine mists of blood into the air, speckling Charlie's face and shirt as she crash-landed against his chest.

"Nina?! NINA!!"

Taking advantage of Quintero's distraction, Cortez stepped out from behind cover and opened fire, landing a clean shot through his right shoulder. Quintero grunted in pain and sent a spray of haphazard bullets in the direction of the agents. Davis, who was stepping out from behind the door to follow Cortez, took one to the leg.

"Uhnnnn…" Davis groaned and dropped to the ground.

Quintero smirked at the fallen agent. Cortez lined up a kill shot.

Bang!

Quintero hit the ground with a dull thud. Cortez immediately dropped to Davis' side.

"I've got you Davis. Let me apply pressure. Just hold on, alright? That backup you ordered is on its way." Cortez tried to joke but knew fear was etched across her face.

"I'm ok..." Davis murmured. He tipped his head and surveyed the scene.

Aki lay in a furry heap. Quintero was in a similar state a few yards away. Charlie rocked and cradled Nina's motionless form. And Savin—

Bang!

Cortez jumped at the gunshot and spun around to see Savin stumble backward, a dark red stain spreading through his shirt, right over his heart. He fired one last disoriented shot into the air and collapsed to the ground. Cortez turned back to find Davis with his gun still raised and trained on Savin.

"He was gonna shoot you."

Cortez was speechless as she stared in amazement at her wounded partner. Davis gave a closer look to the red smears on his gun and hand.

"Is that blood?" Davis mumbled, and promptly passed out.

CHAPTER 14

HONOR, LOVE —— AND FORGIVENESS ——

"I agree, Cortez," Agent Stone said with a curt nod. "Agent Davis absolutely deserves a commendation."

Davis blushed and slid a little further down in his seat. Cortez couldn't help but grin. Davis had yet to adjust to the hero's treatment his colleagues had been giving him in the months since the shooting. And hearing it from Supervisor Stone was absolutely unbearable for him.

"You've both done an exemplary job. Because of you, Quintero's entire operation has been taken down, drugs, firearms." Stone gave Cortez the smallest of smiles. "Your tenacity paid off." I'd quite like to meet with you later in the week to discuss your future advancement here at the FBI. That is, if that's something you're interested in."

Cortez responded quickly. "Abso-yes ma'am-- I mean, absolutely. Yes ma'am. Thank you… But…" Davis snapped his head toward Cortez. "I have to say that we should not forget that Davis here, and I also took down the *entire Dog fighting ring*." For a moment, there was silence in the room. "and with help from our associates and the Human Society we found homes and rehabilitation for all of the surviving animals." Cortez took a deep breath in and pulled Davis up to his feet to stand next to her.

Agent Stone smiled. "Yes you sure did. Great job."

It was Davis' turn to grin and nudge Cortez pointedly with his foot. Agent Stone began to clap and then the entire room erupted in applause.

***

Charlie, sitting alone on the beach, studied the surf. Next to him, resting in the sand was his incredible All-Wood Surfboard that he made himself, like his mentor. The one he had been working on when he met Nina. His eyes were closed as he listened to the surf. He took a deep breath in, and then opened his eyes to scan the ocean. Clean waves swelled and broke perfectly. Charlie stood up as someone called out behind him.

"Looks like a great day to test out a new board."

Charlie turned and watched Nina walking toward him, carrying her Eagle Surfboard under her arm. *He could see Aki trotting by her side as always.*

"Yep. The surf looks good. And so do you..."

Charlie wrapped his arms around Nina.

"Are you sure you're ready for this?" Nina asked as she glanced out to the sea.

She didn't mean to hover, but Charlie's ability to acknowledge the severity of his knee injury had proved dubious time and time again. A smile tugged at Charlie's lips as he gazed back at her. Thinking about it, Nina realized there was hardly ever a time Charlie wasn't smiling when he looked at her. He reached down to finish fastening the bottom strap of his new knee brace before answering.

"I'm ready. I was born ready. Just lost some of that readiness for a moment there and now I'm ready again."

Nina rolled her eyes teasingly, but couldn't stop herself from smiling back.

Charlie and Nina were quiet for a moment as they watched the sea. Finally, Nina spoke.

"Thank you."

"For what?"

"For everything... for believing in me." Nina softly touched his shoulder.

Charlie looked deep into Nina's beautiful eyes.

"You saved my life." Charlie paused. "Nina?"

"Yes?"

"I...I love you..." Charlie studied the sand as he spoke, digging a hole with his toe. Nina felt lightheaded at the statement, but in a good way. She could feel a rush coursing through her vein and she leaned on her tiptoes to give Charlie a kiss on the cheek.

"I love you too… so very much…"

Charlie leaned in to kissed her gently. Their kiss lingered.

"I think he is saying… thank you for rescuing him…" Charlie whispered.

Nina's eyes teared up, as she looked up to the sky.

"Aki…. *you* rescued *me*… love you buddy."

"He was a really good dog." Charlie added.

They turned their focus back to the sea. It was just Charlie and Nina standing alone on the beach. Aki wasn't *really* there. *Or was he?* Nina could *always* feel his presence.

The sky was clear, the waves were rolling perfectly and the breeze was gentle and warm. The sun gleamed off of the two surfboards before them: Charlie's gorgeous, all-wood, golden surfboard with a sun emblazoned on it, and Nina's light blue, hand-me-down, feather adorned board.

Finally, Nina asked him again, "Your knee ok? You got this?"

Charlie tapped his new brace. "I got this… But, how about *you*? You ready?"

Nina could see the honest concern he had for her in his eyes.

She subconsciously raised her hand to run her fingers over the fresh scars that flecked her abdomen. She had initially bought a bathing suit that covered them up, but she couldn't stand to hide any part of herself now. Not anymore.

"I was born on a Navajo reservation in the middle of the desert, not an ocean in sight. Of course, this is easy! Haha!" Nina joked back. Truthfully, she was a little apprehensive, but Nina had made the decision to stop letting fear dictate how she lived her life the day she was discharged from the hospital.

"After you," Nina said and gestured to the ocean. "Show us how it's done Mr. Surfer man."

Charlie heeded her and scooped up his board. In a few minutes, he had made it out past the wave break and turned the board to face back to shore. Charlie took note of an enormous swell pulling in behind him and started paddling furiously. As the wave began to crest, Charlie sprang to his feet with ease. He shot diagonally down the wave, allowing the tunnel to cover him for a moment before darting out of it again.

"How do you feel?" Nina shouted and waved.

Charlie met her eyes, gave her a thumbs-up and called back. "Like I'm riding the best wave ever!"

***

Cortez and Davis could feel that all eyes were on them at the FBI station. Superstar agents. A job well done for sure. After all, they brought down the FBI's Most Wanted, along with their entire operation.

Just as Cortez and Davis started to settle into their glory, Agent Stone interrupted the moment.

"There's just one thing…"

Cortez swallowed hard but kept her face neutral. She could hear Davis' heart beating hard in his chest. He was not yet as adept at remaining calm, or keeping his emotions off of his face, as Cortez was.

"Thanks to your witness, we were able to locate where Quintero stashed the drugs he was attempting to transport in the pickup truck. But I understand the money listed in his ledger as being part of the truck's cargo was never recovered. Any thoughts on that?"

Davis tapped the heel of his shoe rapidly against the floor. Cortez subtly slid her own foot over his and pushed down to hold him steady.

"No ma'am. We found no trace of the money in the car and the witness claims she never saw any cash, only the cocaine."

Stone squinted at Cortez. "…and you believe her?"

"Yes, I do."

Stone shifted her indecipherable gaze from Cortez to Davis and back again.

"…alright then. You're dismissed."

Cortez had to remind herself to breathe again as she and Davis stepped out into the hallway. She slowed to allow Davis to keep pace with her. He had developed a bit of a limp from his wound, but the doctors said it would disappear with time.

"So, case closed, huh?" Davis asked lightly and cast a quick glance Cortez's way."

"Yeeeep. Want to go grab a beer?" Cortez shot back equally as lightly and with just the hint of a smile.

CHAPTER 15

— RETRIBUTION —

The postman wasn't accustomed to carrying such heavy packages across the reservation, and as such, was a little grumpy by the time he arrived at his destination. He knocked sharply on the door of the rundown one-bedroom house and huffed when the owner was not prompt to answer. Eventually a petite, older Navajo woman came to the door.

"Are you Katera Locklear?"

"Why, yes I am."

The postman handed her the heavy package and began his long walk back to his truck without another word. Katera struggled to carry the package across her kitchen, only just making it to the kitchen table before it slipped from her hand. Upon hitting the table, the box split open, sending cash tumbling everywhere. Katera took a step back, stunned at the enormous sum of cash before her. Then, amongst the wads of bills, she spotted a note. It was short, but enough to make her burst into tears of joy.

Retribution... For you, and our tribe.

Love,

N

***

"Your turn now."

Charlie, covered in salty water and beaming from ear to ear, helped Nina carry her board to the water. In the shallows, Nina straddled the board and then paddled out to the wave break as Charlie had instructed and turned the board around.

Nina took a slow deep breath in. She patted the front of the board, and looked up to the sky again.

"We got this, Aki."

Nina could see it coming now, a medium sized wave that looked like it had just enough heft to propel a small woman and her dog back to shore. Nina paddled quickly as the wave approached. As it reached her, she pushed up from the board and swung her legs underneath her so that she was sitting up in a kneeling position. With a sudden lurch, the wave caught them and launched them back toward the beach. Nina felt the wind rush through her hair. She heard the happy barks of her spirit friend before her. She saw the love of her life beaming at her from the shore.

And just like that, Nina and Aki were flying...

"If you have men who will exclude any of God's creatures from the shelter of compassion and pity, you will have men who will deal likewise with their fellow men."

St. Francis of Assisi, Patron Saint of Animals

———————————————————

LAST WORDS FROM THE AUTHOR

This story was inspired by several actual events combined to build a heart wrenching fast paced dramatic story of an abused Native American woman and the dog she saves from enduring pain and certain death in a dog fighting ring. Cruel dog fighting goes on all around the world and here in the United States and it must be stopped. Native women are murdered more than 10 times the national average. They are going missing at record speed and there isn't enough being done to stop this. We can do better.

For more information, you can research these suggested topics and links: *(The author and publisher have no affiliation with these suggested links.)*

Missing and Murdered Indigenous Women

Native Hope
https://www.nativehope.org/en-us/understanding-the-issue-of-missing-and-murdered-indigenous-women

And to help rescue dogs and other animals in need:
https://www.spcai.org/

ASPCA

https://www.aspca.org/investigations-rescue/dogfighting

LIFE Animal Rescue

https://lifeanimalrescue.org/

TANE MCCLURE

Tane McClure is an award-winning film and television producer, director, writer and editor. Her award-winning productions and collaborations include earning a National Journalism Award for the documentary, *Love Betty White*, the Betty White story, and the nominated *Just Call Me Hef,* the Hugh Hefner story; the Emmy Nominated *Station Fires* for Fox News Television; Best Fantasy Feature award for Trance; as well and many other film festival awards and nominations for the short films Rockstar and *Voyager* 2150.

Tane grew up in the entertainment industry with her father actor Doug McClure, who was best known as "Trampas" on the western series *The Virginian.* Tane became an actress at an early age playing the part of an orphan in *The Virginian* episode: *Small Parades.* Tane has since acted in over 60 films including playing Reese Witherspoon's mom in Legally Blonde. As a RCA Records recording artist singer/songwriter, under the names Tane Cain and Tahnee Cain and Tryanglz, her single *Holdin'* On hit the Billboard top 40 charts. Her music can also be heard on the original Terminator movie soundtrack with the popular cult classic Technoir song *Burning in the Third Degree*.

Tane lives in Agoura, California with her husband and their two dogs, two horses, two goats and a bird! They have one very talented grown daughter who is a film producer now as well. She has a lovely rescued dog named Jack.

As an avid equestrian, and lover of all animals big and small, Tane has made it her mission in life to do everything she can to protect those in need.

"If I can help save just one soul in need, whether it be animal or human. then I have truly done something worthy in this life. In this book, there are two souls that are in desperate need of rescuing. Follow their journey together to find hope, trust and eventually love. May the story of "Rescue Heart"... rescue *your* heart as it did mine." Tane McClure

For more information on Tane McClure:
www.McClureFilms.com

CPSIA information can be obtained
at www.ICGtesting.com
Printed in the USA
BVHW040832040122
625440BV00016B/289/J